Isabelle

A Story in Shots

Isabelle

A Story in Shots

John Berger and Nella Bielski

Arcadia Books
London

Arcadia Books Limited
6–9 Cynthia Street
Islington
London N1 9JF

First published in Great Britain 1998
© John Berger and Nella Bielski 1998

John Berger and Nella Bielski have
asserted their moral right to be identified
as the authors of this work in accordance
with the Copyright, Designs and Patents Act, 1988

A catalogue record for this book is available
from the British Library

ISBN 1–900850–07–9

Arcadia Books are distributed in the USA
by Dufour Editions, Chester Springs, PA 19425–0007

We would like to thank Hugh Brody, with whom we watched
many night skies during the writing of this story.

N.B. and J.B.

Typeset in Century Schoolbook by Northern Phototypesetting Co. Ltd, Bolton
Printed and bound in Great Britain by Biddles Ltd, Guildford and King's Lynn

Women and Men in the Story

ISABELLE EBERHARDT, a young woman of Russian nationality, born in Geneva

ALEXANDER TROPHIMOWSKI, called 'Vava'; Isabelle's father

NATHALIE EBERHARDT, formerly wife of the Russian general Count Rostovski; Isabelle's mother. She lives with Vava.

AUGUSTIN ROSTOVSKI, sometimes called 'Tiny', son of Nathalie Eberhardt and General Rostovski, Isabelle's half-brother.

DIMA ROSTOVSKI, nicknamed 'Cactophil'; another half-brother of Isabelle

VERA, a Russian medical student studying in Geneva

LELLA HADRA, an Algerian fortune-teller and peddler

JENNY, Augustin Rostovski's French wife

HÉLÈNE, daughter of Augustin and Jenny; Isabelle's niece

LOUIS HUBERT GONZALVE LYAUTEY, colonel, later general in the French army. First stationed in South-East Asia, he becomes the leading figure in the French conquest of Morocco

EUGÈNE LETORD, an officer on the staff of Lyautey

CAPTAIN FRIOUX, a young officer in the Arab Bureau (Intelligence) of the French army in Algeria

SIDI LACHMI, a sherif of the Quadrya Brotherhood, a religious organization involved in resistance against the French

SLIMAN EHNNI, a sergeant of the Spahis, a contingent of Algerian troops that is part of the French army; Isabelle's husband

CAPTAIN JUNOT, an elderly officer in the Arab Bureau

Act 1

WADI BESIDE AIN SEFRA – ALGERIA – OCTOBER 1904

It is hot, the light is brilliant. A French general is standing among a group of functionaries – some officers, some civilians, journalists, perhaps some local dignitaries. The general's name is Louis Hubert Gonzalve Lyautey.

The wadi is wet and small streams of water are disappearing in the hot sand. Baskets, bundles of clothes and pieces of furniture clutter the foreground. French Legionnaires are searching the desert; they are evenly spaced and move in one direction. Officers direct proceedings. The Legionnaires are picking up scraps from the sand and mud.

> LYAUTEY: I gave them an order to search everywhere, every square metre of sand. They are finding scraps of paper, torn pages. One must always think of posterity.

From a small pile that has been assembled by the legionnaires, the French general picks up a notebook and a muddy revolver. The horizon is barely noticeable, sand and sky blend together.

> LYAUTEY: Otherwise no one will remember us.

LAKESIDE – GENEVA – MORNING, FEBRUARY 1886

The lake of Geneva divides the city in half. On the north side there are small harbours. Due to the exceptional cold, these are partly frozen over. Isabelle, nine years old, is with her half-brother Dima, in his mid teens. She has ventured out onto the thin ice. Gulls circle around her.

Dima, standing on the shore, is trying to persuade her to come back. A few passersby along the promenade glance towards the children.

> DIMA: Isabelle, you're walking on very thin ice! Isabelle, come back!

ISABELLE: It doesn't crack, Cactophil, if you go fast
enough!
DIMA: You're going to drown, Isabelle!
ISABELLE: It's my birthday and I want to go to the
other side.
DIMA: Come back, Is–a–belle!

Dima is joined by a Park Attendant and a Policeman. The
Policeman shouts to Isabelle through a megaphone.

She is a hundred or so yards away. A small crowd has
gathered.

POLICEMAN: It is strictly forbidden to walk on the ice
where you are. . . . Can you hear me. . . . It is
forbidden!

Isabelle waves, as if hearing applause, and continues.
Meanwhile, Vava, Isabelle's father, a large, black-bearded
man in his late forties, has arrived at the shore. He seizes the
megaphone and speaks in a strong Russian accent.

VAVA: Diogenes, my daughter . . . can you hear me?
Today you are nine, Diogenes, and your life
is before you. You haven't learnt enough . . .
come back to us.

For a moment Isabelle is absolutely stationary. Then she
carefully picks her way back towards the quayside and the
waiting crowd.

POLICE STATION – GENEVA

Behind the counter, a Swiss Police Officer is seated at a table,
and a Second Officer is standing by a filing cabinet. Vava
gives the impression that the chair on which he is sitting is
too small for him. Isabelle and Dima are seated side by side
on a bench against the wall. They stare aggressively at the
policemen.

FIRST OFFICER:	She is your daughter?
VAVA:	Correct.
FIRST OFFICER:	Why was she not in school this morning?
VAVA:	She does not go to school.
FIRST OFFICER:	Education is compulsory.
VAVA:	I don't believe in your education of half-truths. I teach her at home.

The Second Officer pulls a file out of his cabinet, and moves in the direction of the First Officer.

FIRST OFFICER:	Can she read and write?
VAVA:	You were thinking of which language, Superintendent?
FIRST OFFICER:	I'm asking if she can write.
VAVA:	In Arabic, in French, in Russian, in Greek – she can write.
FIRST OFFICER:	Mr Trophimowski, up to now I and my colleague have been patient. . . .
VAVA:	Diogenes, write your name for our servant of the people!

She writes in Latin: Isabelle. Then she adds her name below, in Arabic letters.

The Second Officer puts the opened file on the desk in front of the First Officer, who glances at the cover.

SECOND OFFICER:	Another one!
FIRST OFFICER:	Mad Russians, more every year!

The Second Officer runs through the file while showing it to the First Officer. They are both bent over the desk.

SECOND OFFICER:	Alexander Trophimowski, former priest of Russian church . . . member of the World Anarchist Association since 1868 . . . family tutor to the children of General Count Rostovski . . . absconded with General's wife, Nathalie Eberhardt, and her two sons . . . applied for political asylum in the Canton of Geneva in 1875. . . .

5

Isabelle goes over to her father, sits on his knee, plays with his beard. The Second Officer raises his voice.

SECOND OFFICER: . . . uses money obtained from concubine's husband, the aforementioned General Rostovski, to buy Villa Nuova in the village of Meyrin . . . illegitimate daughter born in Cantonal Hospital 1877. . . .

FIRST OFFICER: Listed, since several years, as politically harmless.

GARDEN OF VILLA NUOVA – MEYRIN – AFTERNOON, MAY 1897

The Villa Nuova is a large, neglected, nineteenth-century house. The leaves of unkempt rhododendron bushes glisten in the afternoon sun. In a broken-down summer house, a woman is giggling.

The woman slips furtively away from the pavilion to disappear between the trees. Isabelle, in boots, trousers, and with a spade on her shoulder, walks slowly down the path. She walks like a man. The pavilion has a domed roof, and windows all the way around. Some are broken. A man, dandyish, blue eyes, tall, appears in the doorway. He is Augustin, Isabelle's half-brother.

ISABELLE: You've just fucked her.
AUGUSTIN: You and your foul mouth!
ISABELLE: You and your chicken-brained flirtations. You make me sick, Augustin.
AUGUSTIN: You're jealous, that's all, jealous! And how vulgar it is for a sister to be jealous of her brother.
ISABELLE: Half-brother! I adore it when you play the aristocrat. My Tiny who can't forget he's Count Rostovski!

Isabelle sits down on a bench. She lights a cigarette. Enter Dima, carrying a large cactus and wearing the same clothes as his brother and half-sister. These clothes on the three of

6

them look like Russian peasant uniforms. Dima addresses Augustin and Isabelle, who do not look at him.

> DIMA: As usual, Brother Augustin and Sister Isabelle are discussing their feelings.

Dima pulls out a notebook with a pencil attached, and reads from it.

> DIMA: There are cabbages to thin and plant, pea stalks to gather and cut, tomato plants to water, and the trout pond to be cleaned. An order to pay 934 francs has just been delivered by a bailiff. One shouldn't play cards if one is not lucky at them, Augustin.

An elderly lady comes slowly towards the pavilion, untidily dressed but in clothes that were once elegant. This is Nathalie, mother of Dima, Augustin, and Isabelle.

> NATHALIE: Dima, Dima . . . where is my watering can?
> DIMA: The monthly payment from Father came this morning.
> NATHALIE: Put it in the drawer of my desk, Cactophil. Where is my blue watering can?
> DIMA: I'll show you, Mother. Isabelle, if the pond isn't cleared, the trout will die!

Dima guides his mother towards the kitchen garden.

> AUGUSTIN: One day I am going to make him swallow his bloody cactus.

Vava approaches from the house. Slow, dressed in black. He bends down to tie up the laces of one of his heavy walking boots. He points at Augustin.

> VAVA: There he is! The Count Rostovski who is going to find himself in prison for debt! All decadence is due to the false distinction made between intellectual and manual labour. Leisure should be repose after work,

7

when the body is grateful. . . . Clean out the fish pond!

Meekly, the two grown-up children obey. They throw meal on the water of the pond, and scoop out the fish in large nets with long handles. The fish, as they are pulled out of the water, try to leap back.

ISABELLE:	Let's leave. Let's get the hell out of here.
AUGUSTIN:	The world outside is more ignoble than you think.
ISABELLE:	Ignoble! What a word. We'll go together, Tiny, we'll learn together.
AUGUSTIN:	Back to St Petersburg?
ISABELLE:	To the pyramids, to the Sphinx.
AUGUSTIN:	Dreams!

Isabelle empties a netful of fish into another section of the pond.

ISABELLE:	This family is doomed – I'm telling you, Tiny, for the last time. It has no roots – it is like one of the Cactophil's cactuses.
AUGUSTIN:	The plural is cacti!

NATHALIE'S BEDROOM – VILLA NUOVA, NIGHT

Single bed with brass fittings, lace pillowcases, gilt bedspread – but none of it is very clean. A writing bureau with scattered papers. In a corner several icons on the wall and a lighted candle before them. Nathalie, in her dressing-gown, is seated before a table with playing cards arranged as for a game of solitaire. Also on the table, an oil lamp, turned down low. Vava is seated opposite her.

NATHALIE:	The month's money from our Benefactor has come, my dear.
VAVA:	Benefactor!
NATHALIE:	We'd be lost without General Rostovski's roubles.

8

VAVA:	The Benefactor, as you always call him, pursues us even here.
NATHALIE:	By sending us money?
VAVA:	Through the pitiless laws of heredity – as demonstrated in his and your children!
NATHALIE:	Sometimes, Vava, you seem to forget how once you were my lover, a very passionate lover.

Vava gets up abruptly and goes to the window, perhaps to hide his feelings. Nathalie continues with her game of solitaire.

NATHALIE:	For days now the cards haven't been coming out.

Nathalie sighs, looks at the candle burning by the icons, and speaks as if to herself.

NATHALIE:	Christ aids those who suffer. . . .
VAVA:	In the whole history of the human spirit there has been no greater abomination than Christ.
NATHALIE:	It's not kind of you to make such remarks, Alexander. Without Christ, men would have remained animals.
VAVA:	Men HAVE remained animals.
NATHALIE:	The money's in the drawer. Take it.

Vava pockets the envelope, leaves. Nathalie shuffles the cards.

DINING HALL, VILLA NUOVA

The room in the house where guests meet and talk. Lit by gaslight from the ceiling. The only furniture is a long wooden table with benches. On the wall behind, a large unfinished mural-painting depicting from left to right the Ascent of Man, according to Darwinian theory. The early phases (reptiles, mammals) are complete. Somewhere near the middle, the painting has stopped with Australopithecus Man. The other walls of the room are whitewashed, with signs of damp.

Vava sits at the head of the table, surrounded by Russian emigrés. Among them, Anya with a pince-nez and a stylish mauve dress, a Young Man with a student cap, and Vera, a young medical student. She is wearing a chaste brown frock with a little lace around the collar and sleeves.

ANYA: He was arrested in St Petersburg, in a photography shop off the Haymarket.

YOUNG MAN: Executed the week after Easter . . . twenty-seven years old. Obstinate about two things: Karl Marx and his beard.

ANYA: How many times did I try to tell him? With a beard like that, I told him, you're asking to be picked up. . . .

Enter Isabelle, dressed in her Russian peasant outfit, with a tray of tea cups.

VAVA: What a waste of a life! At the time of Christ, people were waiting for the end of the world; in the Middle Ages they believed in the imminence of the Last Judgement. For you, it's the Revolution that will destroy all evil.

YOUNG MAN: He was twenty-seven!

Vava notices Isabelle. His face lights up.

VAVA: Isabelle, my child!

ANYA: Your daughter!

VAVA: My only child, whom I call Diogenes in the conviction that she will follow the example of that incorruptible philosopher.

ANYA: Why on earth does she dress like a man?

VAVA: I insist upon it. Dressed as a woman she'd be treated as a member of the weaker sex. I want her to be somebody who never hesitates to do what needs to be done. I want nothing to make her weak.

YOUNG MAN: Since the assassination in March, they've recruited thousands of informers. They are everywhere. Not only your concierge, but your shoemaker, your coal merchant. . . .

VERA: How do they make informers? How do they break their pride so easily?

Vera's words are lost in her coughing. Still coughing, she moves away from the table; Isabelle guides her to a bench by the kitchen door. Anya gets up to inspect the painting on the wall.

ANYA: Who is the painter?

ISABELLE: Papa is the painter but he can't finish it: it's a question of faith.

Isabelle arranges a coat around Vera's shoulders.

YOUNG MAN: Things are changing in Russia; perhaps you don't realize it here.

Vera leans her head back against Isabelle's arm, closes her eyes.

ISABELLE: We'll go to the mountains together. . . .

YOUNG MAN: The days of useless self-sacrifice are over.

VERA: When I've passed the exam, we'll go to the mountains . . . not before.

ISABELLE'S ROOM, VILLA NUOVA

The room is austere and untidy. A narrow bed without a pillow. A large table covered with notebooks and pages of writing. On one of the walls, a painting of a minaret. Beside the painting, a mirror. Isabelle, in her nightdress, gets up from the table and takes a white cloth out of a drawer and, in front of the mirror, puts it on like a turban.

Through the window, the cry of an owl. Furtively, the door opens. In the mirror, Isabelle sees Augustin, a little drunk. He is wearing a suit, white shirt, black silk scarf. He smiles.

11

ISABELLE: It's almost morning.

AUGUSTIN: Here's all I won. My luck's left me. Do you want them?

He comes up behind her and places a bank note on each of her shoulders. She shrugs her shoulders so the notes fall.

ISABELLE: Do you like my turban?

He adjusts her headdress and glances idly at some of the written papers on the table. He holds up a page, reading out loud.

AUGUSTIN: 'My dear Eugène, I feel in my heart that I have loved you for so long, since long, long before God created the world.'

Isabelle, furious, pushes him away from the table and tries to seize the letter.

ISABELLE: You dare to read my letters! Who do you think you are!

Augustin jumps on to and off the bed, still holding the letter.

AUGUSTIN: 'Since long, long before God created the world . . . I feel in my heart that I have loved you. . . .'

Isabelle finally grabs the letter and slaps his face. He takes her in his arms.

ISABELLE: You remember, I told you about his advertisement in the French newspaper. 'French officer in the Sahara, bored to death, would like to correspond with a young lady in Europe.' He's been writing to me for a year. I've never seen him. He's stationed in El Oued.

AUGUSTIN: And he's called Eugène?

12

ISABELLE: Eugène Letard . . . Tiny, you are jealous,
          aren't you? Yet there's no reason; you are
          still the love of my life.

She kisses him on the mouth.

COUNTRYSIDE NEAR VILLA NUOVA – SUMMER MORNING

Isabelle, dressed in her Russian peasant clothes, and her
father are on horseback. Both are holding open books in their
hands. The horses walk side by side; she is listening to her
father.

VAVA: The man who first discovered tuberculosis to
          be infectious was Avicenna in the tenth
          century. What was his Islamic name?
ISABELLE: Ibn Sina.

As she answers, she triumphantly spurs her horse and
gallops off, then she reins in and waits for her father, trotting
to join her.

VAVA: Your essay was better than last week. But if
          you are going to talk about treachery, you
          must insist on how treachery is
          Shakespeare's favourite theme. Love
          between two, treachery between many! This
          was his vision. In every play he shows us
          treachery. We'll read Act I, Scene 4, of *King
          Lear* together.

They approach the house. Isabelle dismounts and holds her
father's horse for him.

VAVA: I'll get our Shakespeare.

On his way to the house, he stops to tie up a lace. Isabelle
watches him tenderly.

VAVA'S STUDY, VILLA NUOVA

Bookcases to the ceiling. A single sofa-bed. A large sepia portrait of Tolstoi. Many plants in pots. Augustin is standing on tiptoe by the bed, looking for something on the top bookshelf. Suddenly the door opens. It is Vava. Augustin jumps off the bed and looks guilty.

> VAVA: You bastard! You'd steal from your own mother to pay for your filthy gambling.
> AUGUSTIN: I needed . . .
> VAVA: Liar!

Vava seizes Augustin by the collar and shakes him.

> VAVA: It's not money! No. No! It's names, my God. Names!

Vava hits Augustin.

> VAVA: You're looking for names. You're spying for the Czar!

Vava throws Augustin to the floor. Augustin scarcely resists. The older man sits on top of him, seizes his shoulders, bangs his head against the floor.

> VAVA: I want the truth! Do you hear me? The truth.
> AUGUSTIN: Isabelle! Isabelle! He's gone mad.
> VAVA: Judas!

Nathalie enters in her dressing-gown, hair loose.

> NATHALIE: Stop it, Alexander, I beg you to stop it. Stop!
> VAVA: Do you know what the Benefactor's son was doing? Tell your mother! Tell it!
> NATHALIE: My God. My God . . . you will kill him.

Nathalie collapses and crawls towards the sofa.

> AUGUSTIN: Isabelle! Isabelle!

Isabelle enters, running, and places her hand on Vava's head; he grasps her hand and becomes calm.

ISABELLE: Father, let Tiny get up.

Augustin rises to his feet, wipes the blood from his face. Dima is standing in the doorway.

DIMA: He'd steal money, Father, but not names, not yet . . .

Augustin leaves the room without a word. Nathalie sniffs some smelling salts. Vava leans back in a chair, hands hanging by his sides.

VAVA: We are primitives, Diogenes, primitives because we are among the first. . . . We are clumsy, violent . . . too passionate. Others will come after us who will be better prepared to realize our ideal. History does not advance like a locomotive, but like a glacier. For all the heat of our passion, my beloved, history is cold. So cold. . . .

Nathalie struggles to her feet. Isabelle looks anxiously at Vava slumped in his chair.

DIMA: Go with Mother, I'll stay with him.

Isabelle leads her mother out of the room.

HALLWAY STAIRCASE

On the staircase, Nathalie moans like a child.

NATHALIE: Take me away from here. I can't stand it any more . . . he wanted to kill my son. Take me away, I'll never leave them, but just for a while . . . Take me away for a little while. . . .

SHIP'S CABIN – AT SEA – NIGHT

The cabin is comfortable with two bunks. Hanging objects
swing as the ship rolls. Nathalie is lying fully dressed on her
bunk. Isabelle, in a white dress, is writing in a notebook.
When Nathalie speaks, Isabelle does not immediately look
up; she wants to be left in peace.

> NATHALIE: The first time I saw your father, the coach
> had stopped in front of the house with white
> columns and his overcoat was covered with
> dust. He came to tutor Dima and Augustin.
> The general was away on manoeuvres. . . . I
> fell in love with him at first sight. To love
> like I loved him is terrible . . . one should
> never love like that, one should never go
> away, one should never leave . . . one should
> stay.

Isabelle puts aside her notebook and speaks as if to a child.

> ISABELLE: We'll go back to the Villa Nuova, Mother.
> We're only away for the winter.
> NATHALIE: When people start crossing seas, they never
> come back at the right moment –
> ISABELLE: Don't go on, *Maman*. You need a rest and a
> change.
> NATHALIE: The hot climate in Algeria may not be good
> for my heart.
> ISABELLE: The houses are cool. You don't realize how
> lucky we are to have been lent this house –
> there's a verandah overlooking the sea,
> a well in the garden, palm trees. . . . This
> little house in Bone was meant for us.
> Mektoub!
> NATHALIE: What?
> ISABELLE: Do you know what that means, Mother? It
> means: It has been written.
> NATHALIE: How. . .?
> ISABELLE: When God created the pen he commanded it
> to write. Write down the destiny of all

16

things, he said, all things to the end of the world.

Nathalie is asleep.

SHIP'S DECK

Isabelle descends a metal staircase to the crowded fourth-class deck, where the passengers, almost all of them North African, have improvised shelters against the wind and are sitting or sprawling on the deck. Many of the women are veiled. Some of the men are smoking narghiles. An unveiled woman, over fifty, wearing earrings and bracelets, holds out her hand as Isabelle passes. It could be the gesture of a beggar; Isabelle takes it as such and modestly looks for a coin. As she does so, she says in Arabic: 'Allahou Akbar!' The woman clasps Isabelle's hand to invite her to sit down beside her. Her name is Lella Hadra.

LELLA HADRA: Stay. What I have to tell you is for your two
             ears, not for the brass ear of money. In the
             poor mountains there lived a Bedouin
             shepherd girl called Smina. One day a
             French officer, a Roumi, asked her for water
             to give to his horse to drink. This Roumi
             officer fell in love with Smina – her eyes
             were like damsons. She said she could love
             him only if he became a Muslim. . . . He took
             the oath and she named him Mabrouk.
             Smina's love for her Mabrouk was blind, yet
             she knew he would leave her. 'Next week I
             must go,' he said. 'I will come back soon.'
             And she replied: 'You want me no more,
             Mabrouk, you want to keep neither me nor
             your own word.'

Isabelle sips a glass of mint tea that has been offered to her.

LELLA HADRA: He left to become a major in his army, and
             he married a Roumia as all Roumis do.
    ISABELLE: And Smina?

17

LELLA HADRA:	She remained faithful to her love, she danced in cabarets, she became a camp-follower. She waits for her master to come back. . . . When he comes back she will tell him he is a dog, a son of a bitch, who can love neither word nor woman, and as she says this her eyes – all wrinkled now – will . . .
ISABELLE:	Will?
LELLA HADRA:	. . . will look upon the life they never lived.

BACKSTREET – BONE, ALGERIA – AFTERNOON

The Arab quarter. Barefoot children, women in black robes, mostly veiled. Merchants. Beggars. Isabelle is dressed in a white burnous and a turban. Stops before a small moorish cafe, peers through the bead curtains. In an alcove a group of Foreign Legionnaires sprawling on carpets on the floor. An Arab flute player. A boy serving coffee. Several empty tables. Seated at one is Lella Hadra. Isabelle enters. The habitués glance at her only for a moment – they take her to be an unknown Arab boy.

ISABELLE:	Why did you tell me the story of Smina?

Lella recognizes her voice.

LELLA:	Because a word said is a word given.

Lella is wearing more bracelets than on the boat, and a silver-threaded headscarf. She uses this cafe as her office. She foresees the future, undoes spells, and sells *dawamesk* (a pastry containing cannabis). On the table in front of her are envelopes and small packets of *dawamesk*.

ISABELLE:	Is there nothing more written for me?
LELLA:	Everything is written, but not everything can be read at once. You must return.

Isabelle takes out a cigarette, has no light. Lella nods in the direction of the Legionnaires. A Legionnaire strikes a match.

LEGIONNAIRE:	I knew a man from Bou Saada who tried to light a cigarette with a pistol shot. He blinded himself.
ISABELLE:	The disadvantages of being alone!
LEGIONNAIRE:	You've seen the old woman's pastries? Spread with happiness those ones are....

Isabelle takes two *dawamesk*. Lella refuses any money. Isabelle lies on the carpet near the Legionnaires.

ISABELLE:	I want to go to El Oued.
LEGIONNAIRE:	What's your name?
ISABELLE:	Mahmoud. I come from Tunis.
LEGIONNAIRE:	Bring us a pastry and we'll tell you about El Oued.

The Arab flute continues. Isabelle slips into the arms of a Legionnaire, pulls his face towards her and kisses him on the mouth. He is surprised to discover that she is a woman.

Lella observes the scene. With a small kerchief she wipes her cheek.

TERRACE OF SMALL HOUSE – BONE – EARLY MORNING

Winter sunlight. Nathalie is scattering bread crumbs for birds along the balustrade. Then, wrapped in a blanket, she lies in a deck-chair with her feet up. On the table beside her is a glass of tea. She closes her eyes. Her face is drawn.

Isabelle appears in the doorway that opens onto the terrace from the living room. She is wearing her male Arab clothes She has removed her sandals; her feet are dirty.

NATHALIE:	You've been out all night, my child.
ISABELLE:	How are you, Mother?
NATHALIE:	I couldn't sleep.

19

Isabelle sits on the floor beside the deck-chair and rests her head on her mother's lap.

NATHALIE: I'm worried about you, you're not looking well. And why do you dress like this every night?

ISABELLE: Do you know what I call you when I can't see you, Mother? I call you my White Angel.

NATHALIE: Your breath smells of drink . . . and you are my youngest.

ISABELLE: I'm older than any of you think.

Isabelle moves away from the deck-chair and lies down on the terrace, looking up at the sky.

NATHALIE: Every night you disappear.

ISABELLE: We're going to leave this wretched, small-minded Bone, Mother. We're going to go to El Oued!

NATHALIE: It's not as if this were our own country.

ISABELLE: We'll learn how to live on this earth. . . .

NATHALIE: The General was kind to me, you know that? He was tolerant, he was so tolerant. . . .

ISABELLE: Sleep, Mother, sleep.

Both fall asleep. One on the ground; one in the deck-chair. Pigeons alight on the balustrade and eat the bread crumbs.

SAME TERRACE AT MIDDAY

An Algerian woman servant opens the French windows onto the terrace. Isabelle and Nathalie are still asleep. Putting down her tray, the servant goes over to the deck-chair and says: 'Madame.' She touches the shoulder of the old lady. Silence. Then the servant screams. Nothing stirs. Not even Isabelle. Nathalie is dead.

DINING HALL, VILLA NUOVA – AFTERNOON

Outside, the trees are heavy with snow. Vava, visibly older, with unkempt beard, a blanket over his shoulders, is working on his mural painting, adding flowers along the lower edge. Dima crosses the room, wearing gloves and overcoat. He is carrying a large cactus in a pot, which obliges him to walk with his chin held high, as if blind to everything around him. Isabelle, wearing Vera's student frock, is curled up in a corner on the floor. Her sobs become louder. Vava puts down his brushes.

ISABELLE: Without her I don't want to live!

Vava opens the drawer of the table and takes out a revolver, a nickel-plated six-chamber Colt with an inset ivory handpiece. He loads it.

VAVA: Stand up!

Isabelle gets to her feet and stands at the far end of the long table. Vava walks slowly towards her, holding out the revolver, muzzle towards himself.

VAVA: So you don't want to live? One should always be clear about what one wants! To choose is to be free.

He places the revolver on the table in front of Isabelle. She lowers her hands from her face and stares at the weapon. Nobody moves or speaks. Isabelle begins to laugh. Dima approaches the table, picks up the revolver, and blows lightly across its mouth as if to get rid of a cobweb. When he replaces it on the table, Isabelle picks it up.

Then she notices Vava. The old man's eyes are filled with tears.

ISABELLE: It will be all right, Father. All right. I promise.

GARDEN OF VILLA NUOVA – MORNING

Blue sky above the snow. A suitcase stands by the fish pond. Isabelle, wearing an overcoat, is testing the strength of the ice with her foot. Tentatively she tries her weight. Sure of herself, she runs and slides, as she did as a child.

Dima emerges from behind a shack and watches. Suddenly her feet slip and she falls. She tries to get up, and cannot.

> DIMA: She was my mother just as she was yours. . . .
> She loved you but she trusted me. One by one
> you all go. If you hadn't taken her to Bone,
> she would still be alive. . . .

Isabelle turns, still sitting on the ice, to face him. With her hand she shields her eyes from the sun.

> ISABELLE: It's too late, Cactophil . . . all we can do now
> is mourn.

Dima shouts, partly to bridge the distance, partly in rage.

> DIMA: You all leave and you don't even know where
> and why you're going . . . you're going to
> your ruin. Look at Brother Augustin, eking
> out a living in Marseille and married to a
> shopkeeper's daughter who is nibbling him
> away, crumb by crumb. . . . And you – why
> don't you fill your notebooks with your poetic
> dreams here, in the only house that will ever
> be yours, instead of trying to live them out
> in the murderous world? Vava can still make
> it from his bed to his books. He couldn't
> survive a day by himself. Every night he
> takes morphine, more and more. I should
> know because I get it for him. Sometimes
> he's doubled up with pain.

Isabelle approaches her brother over the ice and kisses him on both cheeks.

> DIMA: Without you, we'll both die . . . there'll be no
> more sense in this house.

Isabelle picks up her suitcase.

ISABELLE: Forgive me, Dima, forgive me. I can't help it. I have to go.

DIMA: Do you know what you're looking for? You're looking for a garden, aren't you? and there's one right here!

Original line drawing by Isabelle Eberhardt

Act 2

MARSEILLE DOCKS – LATE AFTERNOON, SEPTEMBER 1898

Cranes. Derricks. Train wagons. Horses. From the hold of the nearest ship a dozen longshoremen carry sacks of beans down a gangplank and across the cobbles to a train wagon. The file is made up of Europeans and North Africans. All wear similar European work-clothes, the North Africans distinguished by their turbans. Among them, dressed as a man, is Isabelle.

As she descends the gangplank with a heavy sack across her shoulders, the Arab in front of her, on reaching the cobbled quayside, lowers his sack to the ground, takes two steps to the side and prostrates himself to recite a prayer. Isabelle hesitates. Should she warn the man? The Italian docker behind slaps her on the shoulder and they continue with their sacks towards the wagon. The Foreman, holding a wad of invoices, hurries towards the Arab.

> FOREMAN: What the hell do you think you're doing? Who gave you permission? You're in France now. In France we work, we don't pray while working. When we pray, we go to church, and when we work, you son of a whore, we work!

The man gets to his feet. The others who have unloaded their sacks are returning to the ship. Isabelle turns around and slaps her arm in an obscene gesture at the foreman.

TENEMENT KITCHEN – MARSEILLE – NIGHT

The room is ill-lit. Laundry hangs over the stove. Augustin is sitting at the kitchen table. Spread out on the table are conches and other seashells. He is gluing these together to make ornaments to sell to sailors and tourists.

Jenny, his wife, is in a dressing-gown. She has a buxom figure, a small mouth and shrill voice. She is feeling the laundry with her hand.

JENNY: With this goddamned cold, it'll never dry! I need it to change Baby in the morning. And you, what do you care? You and your seashells. Why don't you try selling insurance like my friend suggested?

AUGUSTIN: I'd rather go back and work on the docks than do that.

JENNY: Too proud?

AUGUSTIN: I've never seen such a small shell as this one.

JENNY: Ah! You aristocrat! And now there are two of you. Little sister turns up, all smiles and kisses, and without a penny to her name. Eats every evening, scribbles every night, smokes kif and never lifts a finger to help in the kitchen. You are both the same: you think the world owes you a living!

AUGUSTIN: I sell my shells.

JENNY: One doesn't even know if she's a man or woman. Fish or fowl.

AUGUSTIN: The eye of the hermit crab is the most primitive in the whole history of evolution. Only forty cones.

JENNY: Cones!

Isabelle, in her work clothes, comes in. She unwinds her scarf. Her face and hands are very dirty. Taking some money out of her pocket, she is about to place it on the table.

JENNY: Don't touch that cloth with your filthy hands!

Isabelle, with the gesture of a conjuror, lets the banknotes and coins fall one by one onto the tablecloth.

ISABELLE: What's wrong with the mistress of the house today? It's clean money!

Jenny leaves to attend to the baby in the next room. She slams the door behind her.

AUGUSTIN: There's a letter for you.

30

ISABELLE: Where from?

AUGUSTIN: Algeria.

Isabelle unbuttons her shirt to wash at the sink. Augustin
turns the envelope over.

AUGUSTIN: It's from your postal lover – the Lieutenant!

Isabelle is washing under the tap. Augustin looks intently at
her naked torso and picks up a seashell.

AUGUSTIN: Shellfish, unlike us, are never homeless. You
have beautiful breasts.

Isabelle turns around from the sink and sadly shakes her
head.

ISABELLE: Do you think you've made a mistake, Tiny,
about your home?

AUGUSTIN: Life is a mistake, little sister.

Jenny comes into the kitchen to get a diaper. She eyes the
two of them with suspicion and leaves.

ISABELLE: Read me Eugène's letter.

Augustin opens the envelope with a paperknife.

AUGUSTIN: It's short. He calls you his Gazelle. He's left
El Oued and he invites you to Bone, where
he's now stationed.

Isabelle laughs. Augustin fingers another shell.

'BAR IDEAL' – MARSEILLE – NIGHT

Large wooden tables, and around one of them, already
drinking, a group of Longshoremen and Fishermen. They
make signs for Isabelle to join them. They know her as
Mahmoud from Tunis.

31

FISHERMAN: You can try a different jetty, he's always there, King Rat, and he doesn't live on board, he lives on land. One day I say to myself, I've had enough of this. So, I throw King Rat nothing. I ignore him. He waits one minute, he gives a sign to his gang of rats, and they swarm over the deck and over the whole catch. Every fish mauled. I had to sell the catch at half-price.

LONGSHOREMAN: In the docks, King Rat walks on two legs. You stop to have a piss and there he is! Sitting up and watching you, and you haven't had time to button up your trousers.

LONGSHOREMAN: The Berry docks Monday next – clean wood, not coal shit like the last lot. If we grease the Rat, there's work guaranteed for four days. What do you say, Mahmoud, are you coming in with us?

By way of reply, Isabelle hands some money to the bartender. A bottle of absinthe arrives with a saucer of sugar. The dockers slap her on her back.

LONGSHOREMAN: And the Berry Docks next Monday? We'll count you in?

ISABELLE: I'm leaving the City of Rats.

LONGSHOREMAN: Who wouldn't?

ISABELLE: Monday I'll be in Algeria.

QUAYSIDE – BONE, ALGERIA – MORNING

A ship has docked. The quayside is crowded with people: porters, customs officials, and those waiting to meet friends or relatives. A band is playing. The passengers descend by two gangways: one for cabin passengers, and the other for the Fourth Class who slept on deck.

The crowd on the dockside is likewise divided: the Europeans are gathered around a tall flagpole with a tricolour; the North Africans form a group apart, near the stern of the ship. The sky is full of gulls.

Nearer the water's edge than most of the Europeans stands a junior officer. This is Captain Eugène Letord. He eyes inquiringly each passenger who comes down the Cabin Class gangway.

By the flagpole stands a senior French officer. This is Colonel Lyautey.

Isabelle, dressed as Mahmoud, has already come down the Fourth Class gangway. She has a bundle slung over her shoulder, walks casually between the boat and the Europeans, cigarette in mouth. Whenever she spots a young officer, she briefly studies his face. Certain Europeans, particularly the women, glance at her with suspicion. Their question can be read on their faces: What does this street-Arab think he is doing staring at us?

Lyautey is following the 'street-Arab' with rapt interest. The well-dressed elderly lady, for whom he was waiting, comes within arms' length before he turns to recognize and greet her.

Meanwhile, Isabelle has identified Eugène and is standing a few yards away, watching him as he studies each passenger coming down the gangway.

ISABELLE: 'Young officer, stationed in the Sahara, bored to death, seeks correspondent.'

Eugène spins around flabbergasted.

ISABELLE: Eugène!
EUGÈNE: Never! It can't be.
ISABELLE: You're even thinner than your handwriting!
EUGÈNE: Isabelle?

Clumsily, shyly, he takes her hand and kisses it. Nothing about this encounter between a young captain and a street-Arab has escaped Lyautey.

EUGÈNE: We must get your luggage.

Isabelle makes a sign to show that she has nothing but the bundle she carries over her shoulder.

> EUGÈNE: Not even a dress?
> ISABELLE: I left everything behind, dresses included. Your Isabelle has gone. You are looking at Mahmoud Essadi, a student of the Koran from Tunis.

She pauses, as if to give them both time to think of who she is under her clothes and without a name.

> ISABELLE: . . . only son of a tailor.
> EUGÈNE: And Isabelle Eberhardt?
> ISABELLE: You have to invent her.

Eugène and Isabelle walk along the quayside, past workers, camels, mules. Their progress is awkward because Isabelle keeps stopping in her tracks to look at him. He is carrying her bundle.

> EUGÈNE: There are so many things I want to ask you. . . .

A child comes up to Eugène to beg. A porter, bent like a jack-knife and carrying an immense pile of leather hides on his back, his face parallel to the ground, passes between them.

AN ARCADE WITH LUXURY SHOPS

On the faces of those who pass the French officer and his street-Arab companion can be read surprise, disapproval, consternation, outrage.

> EUGENE: I've never heard your voice in my life, but when you pronounced my name I knew it was you immediately. It was the voice of your letters, your letters which I've read like music for so many years.

Isabelle stops before a saddler's shop.

ISABELLE:	Do you ride with long or short stirrups?
EUGÈNE:	Not too short.
ISABELLE:	There's a Persian saying: 'As you wear your stirrups out, you ought to understand the world better.' I like that, don't you?
EUGÈNE:	May I take Mahmoud Essadi shopping?
ISABELLE:	What shall we do about his hair?
EUGÈNE:	We'll find him a hat.
ISABELLE:	And when he takes his hat off?
EUGÈNE:	He'll be wearing a wig!

HOTEL BEDROOM – BONE – EARLY EVENING

On the walls hang several large oil paintings depicting Oriental scenes: the bazaar, a harem, a Biblical event.

Everywhere – on the floor, on the bed, on the table, in the armchairs – are packets, cardboard boxes, tissue paper, feminine underclothes, hats, shoes, etc. The door to the bathroom is ajar. Eugène, lolling in a chair, is sipping a pastis and smoking a cigarette. Isabelle is in the bathroom.

EUGÈNE:	Sometimes I used to think I was going to die of boredom here.
ISABELLE:	What did you say?
EUGÈNE:	I said: One dies of boredom in these garrison towns: Bone, Ain Sefra, Batna.
ISABELLE:	Boredom? Why?

The sound of running water stops.

EUGÈNE:	There's nothing to do. Sometimes for days, weeks on end. Not even with 'manoeuvres'. So I smoke kif. It stops you thinking . . . it cradles you . . . a return to childhood. But with you here, all that will change.
ISABELLE:	Kif by itself is nothing. It gets interesting when you mix it with absinthe.
EUGÈNE:	I want you to meet a few people here: Jacques Lacoste – he runs a literary

35

	magazine. Simon Lazare, a poet. I've read them passages from your letters, and they admire your writing.
ISABELLE:	Writing! A writer is someone who betrays his best friend, then writes an immortal page on the nature of treachery.
EUGÈNE:	And above all, I want you to meet Louis Hubert Lyautey.

Isabelle, still in the bathroom, is ruffling the wig, prior to putting it on.

ISABELLE:	Who is Lyautey?
EUGÈNE:	Our great and famous colonel . . . a soldier of genius such as you get once in a century. A man of reason and a romantic. A believer, and what he believes in is action.

Isabelle appears in the doorway, impeccably dressed, coiffed, poised. White dress bordered with lace, white stockings, black shoes. For a moment she stands framed in the doorway, as if posing for Eugene.

ISABELLE:	What is he doing here, your romantic who believes in action?
EUGÈNE:	He's on a visit from Indo-China. He's going to build an empire – of a new kind.
ISABELLE:	A colonel?
EUGÈNE:	I'm certain you'll have a lot to say to each other.

She sweeps some underwear off one of the armchairs and sits on it.

ISABELLE:	Yet another empire. . . . Soon we'll all be dead! Did you know that? Dead! My poor Eugène. Am I easier to read than to be with?

A GARDEN – BONE – EARLY EVENING

Thirty or so guests assembled for a garden party. Algerian

servants. Buffet tables. Food and drink. Exotic plants. A raised terrace at one end of the garden, on which there is a grand piano. At the other end, an animal cage housing birds and zebras.

Eugene guides Isabelle between the standing guests, his hand under her elbow, introducing her. They approach Colonel Lyautey.

LYAUTEY: And so you are the charming Isabelle. Eugene has read me some of your wonderful letters, Isabelle, if I may take the liberty of using your Christian name?

ISABELLE: Already in my life, sir, I have had many names.

LYAUTEY: There are honourable reasons for changing one's name – even one's identity – and there are dishonourable ones. I am certain, my dear Isabelle, that your reasons have always been of the former kind.

ISABELLE: In the end every name is effaced by time and the sand, isn't it?

LYAUTEY: We all want to leave something behind, don't you think?

ISABELLE: So little. Do you dream, sir?

LYAUTEY: Yes, I have a dream, a dream to establish for as long as possible a little order, a little peace.

ISABELLE: Whose peace? The order of what?

EUGÈNE: The Marquise de Chamalliere is here, my Colonel.

LYAUTEY: Our story, Miss Eberhardt – for we both provoke stories, don't we – our story is not yet over.

Eugène presents Isabelle to other guests.

SPORTSMAN: Eugène mentioned that you are a keen horsewoman, Miss Eberhardt. Fast horses are the only good thing they have in this God-forsaken country.

37

An Officer approaches Eugène.

> OFFICER: The Colonel would like to see you for a moment.

Eugène turns to Isabelle.

> EUGÈNE: Duty calls.

A Young Woman approaches Isabelle.

> YOUNG WOMAN: Eugène said you can speak at least five languages.
> ISABELLE: My father was a very good teacher.
> YOUNG WOMAN: Do you like rugs?
> ISABELLE: Rugs?
> YOUNG WOMAN: Prayer mats. I've become absolutely fascinated by them, and we go to the bazaar to buy them. We'd love you to come with us, and with you speaking their lingo, we'll get a bargain.

Someone starts to play a piano. The zebras in the cage raise their heads.

> ELDERLY WOMAN: I hear you are a writer. What kind of books do you write? Romances? Adventure stories?
> ISABELLE: Epitaphs, Madame.

Lamps in the garden are lit. Eugène is seated at the piano. He looks anxiously to see where Isabelle is.

Isabelle is sitting alone in a chair, at the end of the garden. Nearby, a group of officers, a little tipsy; among them, Captain Frioux. They are talking about Isabelle.

> AN OFFICER: They say she is of Russian origin, the daughter of a general in the Czar's army.
> FRIOUX: I can just see Eugène as the son-in-law of a Russian general!

Captain Frioux approaches Isabelle with a gallant gesture.

FRIOUX: May I offer you a glass of champagne?

The Officers perform for her the ritual of 'beheading' one, two, three bottles. With a single blow they cut off the neck of each bottle with a sabre. Froth spurts up and over the table. Captain Frioux offers Isabelle a glass.

VOICE: Ladies and Gentlemen! I have the honour of announcing that Colonel Lyautey has consented to sing for us.

Isabelle sips her champagne and speaks to Captain Frioux.

ISABELLE: Are you stationed in Bone, Captain?
FRIOUX: Just visiting. Tomorrow I have to go south again and hunt down the latest trouble-makers.
ISABELLE: You are in the cavalry?
FRIOUX: Intelligence, Madame, the Arab Bureau. We find out who's pulling the strings. In this case it's the Qadrya.
ISABELLE: The Qadrya?
FRIOUX: Fanatics. You have heard of Emir Abdelkader? He thought he could change the world – until we sent him to Toulon. He was a Qadrya.

The first notes of the piano, played by Eugène. Frioux rejoins the other officers to watch Lyautey.

FRIOUX: In Indo-China he behaves like Julius Caesar, and here he thinks he's Rigoletto.

Lyautey stands very upright beside the piano. His eyes are shut – as though in prayer. He sings a Schubert lieder. The guests compose their faces to listen solemnly.

Isabelle, glass in hand, listens to the quavering voice. Everyone's back is turned to her. She studies Lyautey, lost in thought. Then she sighs and, with a single gesture, removes her wig, rubs her hair and lights a cigarette. An Algerian waiter is watching her.

ISABELLE: Is it always like this when they give a party?

The waiter shrugs his shoulders.

ISABELLE: From the back of the garden, can you get out into the street?

The waiter explains with gestures. Isabelle thanks him in Arabic.

Lyautey is enchanted by the music and by the attention of his audience. Eugène, while accompanying him on the piano, sees Isabelle leave through the back door. Lyautey reaches the last tremulously held note. Clapping. Cries of 'Encore!'

HOTEL BEDROOM – BONE – MORNING

Isabelle is sorting out her bundle of possessions. Wearing her Arab man's trousers and a cotton shirt, she is standing barefoot at a small round table. In front of her, spread on this table, are her notebooks, a bundle of letters, a djellaba and, wrapped in a beaded cloth, her revolver. She takes some of these things and arranges them in the drawer of the dressing table. She picks up a burnous and begins to move across the room.

She approaches one of the oil paintings: a portrayal of a holy man – more from the Bible than the Koran. Isabelle peers at it and then wraps the burnous around her head, in a parody of the portrait. Then she takes the burnous and drapes it over the painting.

FRENCH ARMY HEADQUARTERS – BONE – DAWN

Eugène is running up a wide staircase. An old woman is washing the stairs.

Eugène pulls off his gloves and knocks lightly on a massive door with brass fittings. Enters. A large room with bookcases.

The blinds are down so that only a little light filters in. Lyautey is seated at a table with breakfast, fruit, a vase of flowers, on a white tablecloth. He is wearing an embroidered dressing-gown over elegant pyjamas. On the table there is one unusual object: a gas burner with a flame at its tip. (Like a laboratory Bunsen burner but taller, more delicate and made of brass.)

Before Eugène arrived, Lyautey was reading a report. Now he takes off his glasses, beckons his friend to sit down, and lights a cigarette from the 'eternal flame' of the burner.

LYAUTEY: I've always liked conversations over breakfast. So did your father. The milk's there. Our friend the other evening at the garden party, Miss Eberhardt, is a remarkable person. I offer you my congratulations.

Eugène shifts in his chair. Lyautey offers him a cigarette from a gold case, and indicates the 'eternal flame'.

LYAUTEY: In any case, it's the future I want to talk about. Now your father is dead, I feel I owe it to him to keep an eye on you.

Lyautey stands up and comes behind Eugène to place a hand on his shoulder.

LYAUTEY: You are wasting your life here. You are living with clichés, military clichés, ethical clichés. In Indo-China, by contrast, we're making history. You would discover yourself with us out there, and you would live a life dedicated to . . . well, to something!

Lyautey strolls to the window and opens the blinds.

LYAUTEY: Another sunny day. Well, there's my offer, Eugène. Come to Indo-China. Come with us.

Eugène puts on his gloves. He is silent.

41

HOTEL BEDROOM – BONE – AFTERNOON

Eugène reclines dreamily in a steaming bath. Isabelle enters, barefoot, tousled, wearing her brown student frock.

> EUGÈNE: You're dressed already! I've never seen that frock.

Isabelle kneels down by the bath.

> ISABELLE: I inherited it from a friend. Her name was Vera. She came from a small town in Russia and was studying medicine in Geneva.

Eugène stands up in the bath. Isabelle drapes the elaborate Turkish towels around him. While doing so, she talks.

> ISABELLE: Vera wanted to be a doctor. Her life was determined by this one thought, this one desire, to help people. She was near the end of her studies . . . and she had tuberculosis. The exams were in October. By the end of September she couldn't even get out of bed. Every morning she asked me what date it was and made me promise that, on the day, I would take her to the exam. She died two days before she was due to take it. She was herself, until the last moment, truly herself.

They slowly walk into the bedroom. Eugène, wrapped in his towels, takes her into his arms.

> EUGÈNE: Do you think I live with clichés?
> ISABELLE: Why?
> EUGÈNE: Here we're boxed in with clichés, everyday clichés, ethical clichés. Let us get away. I've thought out a plan for us. I want to leave the military. We could go to Quebec. It is the France of the coming century, and more than twice as large.
> ISABELLE: No, Eugène, you don't understand.

She frees herself from his embrace. He sits down on the bed.

> EUGÈNE: We'll discover a new world together, build our home, bring up our children.

Isabelle picks up his boots, tunic and kepi from the floor.

> EUGÈNE: There'll be no more compromises.
> ISABELLE: Quebec! What is it? A bit of France, a bit of Europe in yet another colony.
> EUGÈNE: I thought this is what you wanted.

Isabelle abruptly throws all his uniform out of the door into the corridor.

> ISABELLE: I know what I don't want. I know what I have to get away from!

Minutes pass in silence. There is a knock on the door, Isabelle opens it. A hotel Servant, with Eugène's tunic over his arm.

> SERVANT: The boots will be cleaned. Do you want the tunic pressed, Madame?

Isabelle takes the tunic from the servant. Eugène is still on the bed. Isabelle holds the uniform in front of her.

> ISABELLE: You all dream of the Great Civilisation! I can't see an order worth imposing. Whatever I'm looking for, I'll find it beyond your frontiers. If I find it anywhere, it will be in the wilderness, my wilderness, if I find it . . .

HOUSE OF A WEALTHY MERCHANT – BONE – AFTERNOON

A number of French officials have been invited to a reception by a wealthy merchant. Coffee and pastries are being served, and the host is making a speech to his guests in a room which gives onto a terrace. During the host's speech, Lyautey wanders onto the terrace. The terrace overlooks the outer courtyard of a small mosque, where there is an arcade and a fountain. Seated on a carpet in the courtyard, an old Arab is instructing three others sitting before him. One of the three is Isabelle, dressed as Mahmoud. Lyautey beckons to somebody in the room. Eugène comes out and Lyautey indicates to him the courtyard of the mosque.

LYAUTEY: Our student of the Koran has fascinating connections. No play-acting there.
EUGÈNE: She lives each moment as if it were her last.

The four Arabs below are reciting from the first chapter of the Koran.

VOICES: 'In the name of God who is Good and Merciful, praise to God . . . Lord of the Day of Judgement . . . it is You alone we adore, from You alone that we ask . . .'
LYAUTEY: Are you really sure she is a woman?
EUGÈNE: Yes, I'm sure.
LYAUTEY: And supposing, Eugène, you had come to know – by what shall we call them? The same disclosures? – that our student of the Koran was a man: would you be willing to tell me?
EUGÈNE: Isabelle is a woman.

They both look down from the balustrade at the courtyard. They turn around when a Servant offers them coffee on a silver tray.

LYAUTEY: It's a difficult choice for you, I know. It's between two kinds of freedom, isn't it? Ours, which comes with the flag and depends upon discipline and order. And hers, which is the thoughtless freedom of the nomad.
EUGÈNE: Thoughtless? If only I knew half what she knows.
LYAUTEY: Nobody, my dear boy, will ever be able to share her freedom with her.

44

OUTER COURTYARD OF MOSQUE

Eugène enters the courtyard, searching for Isabelle. Finally he spots her sitting at the mosque's fountain, washing her feet. Isabelle looks up.

ISABELLE: What's the matter, Eugène?

EUGÈNE: I have to leave. I've been posted to Indo-China. Tonkin.

ISABELLE: It's Lyautey who is taking you?

EUGÈNE: I didn't want to go, it all happened so quickly and now . . . I have to leave. I didn't have the courage to tell you face to face . . . your eyes make me feel like a coward.

ISABELLE: A coward! You're out of your mind.

EUGÈNE: I'll write to you.

ISABELLE: We've written so many letters to each other, haven't we? So many . . . I'm leaving too. I'm leaving for the south. Perhaps I'm better in letters.

TERMINUS OF A RAILWAY LINE – DESERT – MORNING

In front of a train is a huddle of Arab passengers. Others are off-loading luggage. Several camels and their nomad herders sit on the ground.

Isabelle walks over to the men by the camels. The train backs out along the single line. Steam and smoke hang in the air, then begin to drift away. A vast desert landscape with dunes spreading towards the horizon.

There is no station; the train stopped at the track's end.

Isabelle sits down on a saddle. A Camel Driver addresses her.

CAMEL DRIVER: Where have you come from?

ISABELLE: From Tunis. And you?

CAMEL DRIVER: El Oued.

ISABELLE: I'm going to El Oued.

CAMEL DRIVER: You go to Bordy Saada and from there to Bir Sthil and from there to El Mraiev and from there to El Magger and from El Magger to Touggourt, in Touggourt you get your pass stamped and you go to Temassine, after Temassine to Ferdyenn to Moiet-el-Caid and to Big Ourmes and the next day you arrive in El Oued.

SOUF DESERT – BEFORE SUNSET

Towards one horizon, dunes; towards another, sandy rocks. In a few places scrubs of drinn grass. A small nomad encampment, their wooden-framed tents already pitched for the night. A herd of sheep and goats. Some camels hobbled behind the tents. Near one of the tents an old man is seated, and near him, Isabelle, dressed as Mahmoud, is taking saddle bags off a mule. The Old Nomad is talking, as if almost to himself, but in fact to her.

OLD NOMAD: The Qadrya, my little Tebbib, submit to God and to no one else. For twenty generations, twenty . . . their colour is green, the prophet's colour.

He shows her the green rosary he is wearing around his neck. The old man is blind.

OLD NOMAD: If you want to learn, go to Sidi Lachmi, the marabout of Guemar. He is a sheik and a holy man. The tribes listen to his teachings as do the angels.

Three children approach, each holding a fistful of sand. In turn they pour the sand into the blind man's hands. He feels and weighs each fistful and pronounces.

OLD NOMAD: We're a day's journey west of the Chott of Djerid. There's drinn for the herd an hour to the south.

46

Far away, a rifle shot.

SOUF DESERT – BEFORE SUNSET

A small French convoy: one officer, four spahis on horseback
and two Arab prisoners, wrists bound, on foot. Shots ring out.
Hidden behind the ghourd of a dune, a Young Arab on
horseback fires at the convoy. Then he shouts and another
Arab horseman appears from behind another ghourd. Both
men charge forward, firing from the shoulder.

The Legionnaires leap from their horses and, kneeling,
return the fire. The officer draws his revolver. The prisoners
shout to their liberators. The Second Arab Horseman falls.
The First Horseman charges on and, in turn, is hit. His rifle
drops, but he is able to stay on his horse, which veers away
towards the horizon.

NOMAD ENCAMPMENT – SOUF DESERT – EVENING

The Old Nomad, as before, is seated near a tent, but is now
alone. He recites to himself.

OLD NOMAD: A sandstorm of shots should never give us
fright. Death is God's gift, his porter the
bullets.

A horseman approaches.

HORSEMAN: May the Peace of God be with you.
OLD NOMAD: You are in the hands of God and then in
mine. I will answer for you.

The Horseman slides from his horse to the ground. He is
gravely wounded and has no rifle. He is carried into a tent.

NOMAD'S TENT – NIGHT

The Horseman, laid out on a palliasse, is feverish and

breathes with difficulty. He is covered with a sheepskin. There are two candles alight and many sacks. Isabelle, sitting cross-legged, is swabbing his face with water from a basin. The Old Nomad is also in the tent, listening.

HORSEMAN: We set fire to the village of Marguerite because farm by farm they had seized our land – the Roumis – and face by face they were spitting into our eyes. Nearly a hundred of my brothers were captured. I escaped.

The Horseman winces with pain and grasps Isabelle's arm.

ISABELLE: Do not try to talk.
HORSEMAN: We'll drive them out, force the Roumis back to their own drunk continent.
ISABELLE: Shhhh. Shh.
HORSEMAN: For those on the run, every pool is only as deep as the cat's paw is long. . .

He groans.

Isabelle lifts him up to make him more comfortable. His head falls against her chest.

HORSEMAN: My body tells me you are a woman.

Isabelle bends down and kisses him passionately; he closes his eyes. She sits up.

ISABELLE: Madhourri!

The Horseman is dead.

SOUF DESERT NEAR NOMAD ENCAMPMENT – EARLY MORNING

Sand, sky, distance, all merging. There is an improvised grave. In it, the Horseman's corpse, wrapped in a winding sheet. The Old Nomad with his tentative blind man's fingers is opening the corpse's eyes.

OLD NOMAD: May he now see Heaven, and may the Angels come quickly to question him.

Isabelle, a prisoner between two armed Bedouin Guards, is being led towards the grave. They are holding her brutally. Around the encampment other newly arrived Bedouins with camels and horses.

BEDOUIN: The shit of those who eat with the jackals smells of them.

He prods Isabelle.

One Bedouin unslings his rifle.

Sidi Lachmi climbs the dune and comes towards them. He is wearing a turban of yellow and gold, a green burnous, and filigree riding boots.

BEDOUIN: We've brought you the informer, Sidi Lachmi.

The guard forces Isabelle to her knees.

SIDI LACHMI: Who are you?
ISABELLE: A traveller.
SIDI LACHMI: Where are you from?
ISABELLE: I came through Temmassine to Ferdjenn, through Ferdjenn to Moiet-el-Caid, through Moiet-el-Caid to Big Ourmes.

One of the guards pushes her head down.

SIDI LACHMI: How did you warn the French about the raid on their caravan?
ISABELLE: I didn't.
SIDI LACHMI: Where are you hiding your fear?
ISABELLE: I have none.

Sidi Lachmi makes a sign to the guards to release her.

SIDI LACHMI: Which is your horse?
ISABELLE: As it is written, if there were two horses, one to take me to happiness and the other to unhappiness, I would not choose, I would take the nearest.

Sidi Lachmi beckons to the guards to leave them.

SIDI LACHMI: Where are you going now?
ISABELLE: I want to study with you.
SIDI LACHMI: What have you heard about the Qadrya?

Isabelle fingers her rosary.

ISABELLE: I know your colour is green.

Sidi Lachmi turns his back abruptly.

ZAOUIA – VILLAGE OF QUEMAR – MORNING – WEEKS LATER

The Zaouia, adjoining the mosque, is the religious school of the local group of the Qadrya Brotherhood. Isabelle is kneeling so that her head can be shaved. The shaving finished, the man who is performing the ritual places a coronet on her head and a cloak over her shoulders.

The door to the courtyard is open and two men are watching the ceremony from outside.

YOUNG MAN: The new Khouan is dressed like a man, rides a horse like a man, fires a gun like a man, and answers to a man's name. But the nape of his neck is a woman's.
OLD MAN: When you're older, you'll know the difference between a man and a woman is brief.

PALM GROVE – EL OUED – EARLY AFTERNOON

Across the dunes it is difficult at this hour to distinguish
between the white sand and the light. Date-palms grow
around a man-made saucer-like hollow. On the north rim of
this crater, where the slope down is steepest, stand a horse
and rider.

The rider is Sliman, wearing a turban and gandoura. He is
gazing at another horse and rider who have dismounted
below, near a well amongst the palm trees. The distant figure
is Isabelle. She is washing her body ritually, first the right
side, then the left. She lies down near the well, eyes closed.
Sliman climbs up a palm tree by the well. He gazes down at
Isabelle. His voice speaks, but his lips do not move.

    SLIMAN: You are the hidden rose, the rose of all roses.

Isabelle smiles as if she has heard. Sliman, now standing
over her, speaks with his mouth moving.

    SLIMAN: The Captain sent me to Kouinine. I have to
             be back in barracks before sundown. Why do
             you say nothing? Do you want to make me
             ashamed?

Isabelle opens her eyes.

    ISABELLE: Did you tie up your horse?

There is a small garden beside the well. In it grow carrots,
mint, little peppers, a kind of parsley. Very green. The whole
garden is scarcely larger than a bed, and it is irrigated by a
network of tiny ducts made by hand with plaster. Some of the
ducts have been dammed with coloured rags. The water is
flowing slowly like quick silver.

PALM GROVE – EL OUED – EARLY EVENING

Sliman and Isabelle are lying naked, covered with her
burnous.

SLIMAN:	If the Captain hadn't sent me to Kouinine, I wouldn't have met you.
ISABELLE:	You would have met me anyway: it was arranged before I was born, Sliman.
SLIMAN:	Before birth, we belong to the world of the angels, but you were well and truly born. You are truly here on earth.
ISABELLE:	How do you know that, Sliman?
SLIMAN:	When I kiss your lips and your hands, you want me to kiss your whole body.

OFFICE OF ARAB BUREAU – CONSTANTINE – AFTERNOON

Heavy furniture. New electric fan. A large, decorative aquarium of mediterranean fish. Major Frioux at ease in a chair behind his desk. Frioux has a promising career before him. Opposite him sits Captain Junot, in his fifties, his unexceptional career almost over.

FRIOUX:	I've read your report on the Eberhardt woman. Does she still live with the Spahi you mentioned?
JUNOT:	Yes. Sliman Ehnni, Quartermaster Sergeant 5th Battalion.
FRIOUX:	Can you add anything more?
JUNOT:	They live together in a ruin, and she pays ten francs a month for it. She has run up debts in the souk.
FRIOUX:	Does Sergeant Ehnni belong to the Qadrya?
JUNOT:	No.
FRIOUX:	Is there anything new concerning Eberhardt's relations with the troublemakers?
JUNOT:	All she wants is to sleep with the holy man.
FRIOUX:	Which one?
JUNOT:	Sidi Lachmi.
FRIOUX:	We have a file on him; we'll look at it.
JUNOT:	Don't be deceived by the men's clothes she wears, Major. She'd fuck anyone, Eberhardt.

52

	If she were a Kabyle, we could pack her off to a brothel. She'd get her fill of hot milk there!
FRIOUX:	Be careful not to have a one-track mind, Captain. The Bureau believes that the Eberhardt woman is up to something more dangerous than you seem to be aware of. We believe Eberhardt is a go-between for the Qadrya and the English.
JUNOT:	You'd have to be madder than the English to recruit her as an agent. She can't get enough Arabs into her bed, that's the long and short of it.
FRIOUX:	I want her kept under constant surveillance.

ROOM OF ISABELLE'S HOUSE – EL OUED

The house is on the edge of the town, next to the dunes. There is no furniture in the room. The floor is sand. Hanging on one of the irregular walls, Sliman's Spahi uniform. Isabelle, dressed as an Arab woman, is by the door which opens onto a sand courtyard. She is holding up two threads of cotton towards the feeble light. Sliman is reclining on the floor of the room.

ISABELLE:	How long the days of Ramadan are.
SLIMAN:	The Crocodile has not eaten the sun, so the sun will go down and we'll feast all night.
ISABELLE:	I can bear not drinking and not eating, what's hard is not smoking all day.

Sliman moves towards her, intending to embrace her.

SLIMAN:	It's even harder not to make love.

Isabelle holds him at bay, showing him the two threads.

ISABELLE:	Not until the sun sets, not until–
SLIMAN:	Not until you cannot tell the difference anymore between a white thread and a black thread.

ISABELLE: Let's make the time pass quicker with a
history lesson. Who were the first invaders
of the Maghreb?
SLIMAN: The Phoenicians, the Romans, the Arabs . . .

Sliman begins to caress her ankles.

ISABELLE: No. After the Romans came the Vandals.
SLIMAN: The Vandals?
ISABELLE: How do you ever expect to get out of the
army of the Roumis and find another job – if
you refuse to learn?

He is caressing her knees.

SLIMAN: The sun is going down. It is going down now,
now.
ISABELLE: After the Vandals came the Byzantines, and
after the Byzantines the Arabs.
SLIMAN: Not the Turks?
ISABELLE: No, the Turks were later.

His hand is now between her thighs. Abruptly, in the very
last light, he pulls up her skirt and buries his face in her lap.

SLIMAN: I can no longer tell the difference between a
black thread and a . . .

MARKETPLACE IN GUEMAR – NOON – MONTHS LATER

It is very hot. An amateurish pencil drawing on the lined
page of a notebook. Next to a tethered horse, seated on a
sack, Isabelle is drawing what she can see in front of her
across the open square of dry earth. Behind Isabelle, seated
on a camel saddle, a Bedouin is sewing.

A French lieutenant on horseback rides past, followed by his
retinue. The Bedouin puts down his sewing. He assumes
Isabelle is a man.

BEDOUIN:	He can't sleep at night.
ISABELLE:	Prayer is better than sleep.
BEDOUIN:	I'm talking about the Haken, the Lieutenant. He only falls asleep, according to his servants, when day breaks. Where have you ridden from?
ISABELLE:	El Oued.
BEDOUIN:	Come. I'll show you something it would be a crime to draw.

The Bedouin leads Isabelle to a small yard where there is a line of women, each woman holding a cock in her arms. A man with a knife stands before an upturned wooden box. Each woman reluctantly hands over the bird she has carried. The man slits its throat and throws the carcass onto a pile of others.

BEDOUIN:	Last night, the Lieutenant couldn't sleep. So the Lieutenant has ordered every cock in the encampment to be slaughtered. Tomorrow he'll he able to sleep late.

INNER COURTYARD OF THE ZAOUIA IN GUEMAR – AFTERNOON

Several travellers are waiting to eat, men cooking on open fires. Under the arches of the arcade sit three women veiled in blue. One of these is Sidi Lachmi's wife.

WIFE:	We need more water! And do not forget the oil.

The fires are burning high. Isabelle in her role of Khonan accompanies Sidi Lachmi across the courtyard to a circle of small stone benches. They sit down next to each other on one of the benches and Sidi Lachmi places an open book on his student's knees.

ISABELLE:	We were going to speak today, Sidi Lachmi, about fate.

Sidi Lachmi is searching through the book he put down. He does not reply.

ISABELLE: There is a question. Do those who fight, oppose fate? Can we rewrite the words of the future?

SIDI LACHMI: Our victories are written, our defeats too. But we were to talk of fidelity! Perhaps fidelity begins, also, with the word, the word given.

They are interrupted by the sound of approaching horses and Captain Junot, accompanied by two spahis, enters the courtyard. All eyes turn towards the officer. Sidi Lachmi is obliged to play the host. He stands and makes a stiff gesture.

JUNOT: Where but in the desert can souls who are drawn to each other meet so easily? I love these wide empty spaces, believe me. I envy you. I'd choose the dunes rather than a desk, if I could. I'd choose the dunes.

He sits down on one of the stone benches, takes off his kepi, and wipes the interior with a handkerchief.

JUNOT: I was passing by and wondered whether I could ask for a glass of water. I still have a long way to go.

Sidi Lachmi makes a sign to one of the servants who pours water from a pitcher into a glass.

JUNOT: You are preparing a celebration?

SIDI LACHMI: A simple meal for the travellers who have travelled far.

JUNOT: I heard you had been away yourself.

SIDI LACHMI: No.

The servant brings the glass of water; Junot takes it.

JUNOT: To the south?

SIDI LACHMI:	I would need a special pass to go beyond Toggourt.
JUNOT:	A formality, sherif. But, of course, formalities count. You teachers of the Koran are the first to insist.
ISABELLE:	The formalities of your office, Captain, are addressed to your superiors at Constantine, not to Heaven.

Junot stretches himself and lifts the glass to his lips. Before he starts drinking, he freezes; he stares at a spot near him on the stone bench. A scorpion. He does not dare move or speak. Isabelle gets up and, with an experienced gesture, picks up the insect.

ISABELLE:	The scorpion is concerned about only one thing: to kill as many other beings as possible, because it knows that in the end it will kill itself.

She throws the scorpion into the fire. Junot quickly empties his glass, puts on his kepi, gets up, and leaves without saying a word.

COURTYARD – EL OUED – EVENING

A horse and a well. Isabelle has been washing clothes in an enamel basin by the well. On the sand she has arranged a white sheet on which she lays the washing to dry. A man's shirt spread out. She is putting her washed student frock beside it.

The door to the street suddenly opens. Sliman in his uniform as a spahi. As soon as he sees Isabelle, he slams the door behind him.

SLIMAN:	You were not here yesterday.
ISABELLE:	No, I was not here.
SLIMAN:	I was here.
ISABELLE:	You were here when you were finished at the barracks.
SLIMAN:	You didn't leave a word for me.

ISABELLE:	When I left I didn't know . . . I am yours, Zuizou.
SLIMAN:	You lie when you say you are mine.
ISABELLE:	No.
SLIMAN:	What do you do in the dunes out there?
ISABELLE:	I learn.
SLIMAN:	With the marabout.
ISABELLE:	Yes, and others.
SLIMAN:	I know what you learn. They lust after you, all of them, and you learn to please them.

Isabelle hurls herself at Sliman and starts to beat him with her fists. Not like an hysterical woman, but violently and effectively like a fighter. As she hits, she shouts.

ISABELLE:	You learn nothing! You imagine nothing! You're weak! Why aren't you ashamed to be a soldier in the army of those who've stolen your country?

She tries to tear his tunic off him. He neither steps back nor resists. He stands there like a tree under the rain. Eventually this forces her to stop. She begins to cry.

SLIMAN:	If I say something once, it is true for always. I keep my word and I want to keep you.

Very slowly she edges towards him.

ISABELLE:	Sliman, my love, my Zuizou, O Sliman, my heart, forgive me, please forgive me. I will never hit you again, never, never, you believe me my Zuizou, never again. Say that you believe me, my dove, say that you forgive me, my master.

Silence.

ISABELLE:	I will never hit you again and nothing can part us.

Silence.

OFFICE OF ARAB BUREAU – CONSTANTINE

Major Frioux is dictating to an old French military clerk.
While dictating, he watches a red mullet swimming
backwards and forwards in the aquarium.

> FRIOUX: To Captain Junot, El Oued. In reply to your
> report concerning Isabelle Eberhardt, alias
> Mahmoud Sandi, I hereby inform you that
> the Arab Bureau in Constantine is taking in
> hand all questions raised by her activity in
> the Military Territories. Henceforth all
> initiatives will come from us.

Frioux sprinkles seed into the aquarium for the fish to eat.

MERCHANT'S HOUSE – BEHIMA – A MORNING THE NEXT YEAR

The house is a rich one. Stone floor, wall hangings, silver
trays. Six or seven men are sitting on cushions drinking tea
in a large room with arches that give onto a courtyard, where
there are tamarisk trees. Isabelle enters and sits down next
to Sidi Lachmi.

The two are talking intimately. He whispers into her ear,
rises to his feet and takes off his green burnous. She takes it
and explains to their host, the Merchant.

> ISABELLE: Sidi Lachmi is going to pray. I hear you have
> some letters you'd like me to translate?
> MERCHANT: If you are willing . . .

Isabelle puts on the green burnous of Sidi Lachmi, lights a
cigarette, strides into the yard, beckoning the merchant to
follow. It is by now December and the weather is cold. They
sit on a stone bench under an arcade; Isabelle pulls the cowl
of Lachmi's burnous over her head. She gestures like a robed
judge. The Merchant hands her a letter.

> ISABELLE: 'Paris, 18th December 1900. Dear Sir. . .'

59

A man with a beard enters from the village square. He approaches slowly, eyes to the ground, lost in thought. His name is Abdallah.

ISABELLE: 'Of the 211 sheep shipped to Marseille on October 12th, 107 were found to be suffering from Malta fever . . .'

Abdallah ambles along the arcade, behind Isabelle and the Merchant.

ISABELLE: 'Foreseeing that the meat of the said sheep could under no circumstances receive a selling certificate from the municipal abattoir, we were obliged to sell them on the hoof . . .'

Isabelle pulls the burnous around her shoulders. She is cold.

ISABELLE: '. . . at a quarter of their price to unregistered butchers . . .'

At the end of the arcade a sabre hangs on the wall. Abdallah stares at it. Suddenly he tears it down and, with both arms raised, strikes Isabelle from behind. The sabre is deflected by a wire for drying clothes and hits her shoulder instead of her head. Isabelle falls forward onto her knees. Abdallah is seized by men rushing from every side.

Getting to her feet, Isabelle totters like a sleepwalker, to where the men hold Abdallah. Her gandoura is bloodstained.

ISABELLE: What do you hold against me?
ABDALLAH: I hold nothing against you, you have done nothing to me. I do not know you, but I must kill you.

A Young Man runs into the yard with a rifle.

YOUNG MAN: Let me shoot the dog now!

Sidi Lachmi raises one hand in a gesture of interdiction.

| SIDI LACHMI: | They're waiting for us to kill him, so they can round up every Qadrya they can find. |

The Young Man lowers his rifle.

ABDALLAH:	God told me to do it.
SIDI LACHMI:	Do you know she's a Moslem?
ABDALLAH:	I know she – *she*, as you say – she is a Moslem. God wished me to kill her. God still wishes it.

Sidi Lachmi's Wife, who has been watching with the women of the household, comes forward.

| WIFE: | You're lying! God did not wish it – that's why she is alive. That's why you did not see the wire on which we hang our clothes. That's why the blade did not touch a hair of her head. God did not wish it. How much did they pay you? |

Isabelle collapses.

ISABELLE'S ROOM, HOSPITAL – EL OUED – NIGHT

The windows are shuttered. Bars of light.

It is a military institution. Everything of standard issue. Two narrow metal beds, the second one empty. A shelf above Isabelle's bed, with a jug and tin mug. A small table with bottles.

Isabelle's left shoulder and arm were badly wounded. She suffers spasms of pain, her hand going rigid and clawlike.

The door to the passage swings open. In the doorframe, Dima. He is dressed as he was in Meyrin. He carries a blooming cactus which he places on the table.

He picks up Vava's revolver (it was not on the table a moment ago), and blows across its mouth. He strolls over to the wall

61

facing the bed on which a handwritten page of regulations has been pinned.

> DIMA: 'Sanitary Service Regulations . . .
> Disciplinary punishment which may be
> inflicted on civilian patients . . .'
> Can you be a civilian if you are as alone in
> the world as you are?
> As for Disciplinary Punishment, you have a
> fever of 40.2 centigrade. You have lost the
> use of your left arm. You are penniless.
> Your Sliman has tuberculosis.
> Have you found your garden?
> ISABELLE: Yes.
> DIMA: Do you want to know the end of your story?
> ISABELLE: Stay with me!
> DIMA: You didn't stay. . . .

Dima turns down the blanket of the second bed, removes his shoes, lies down and pulls the bed clothes up to his chin. His head on the pillow is the face of a corpse. Isabelle is asleep.

> ISABELLE: The Cactophil is dead!

Gradually her face becomes calm. Sliman enters. The second bed is empty, there are neither flowers nor revolver on the table. He tiptoes to the bed, calls her name softly. She does not stir. He kisses her above the eyes, walks towards the door, has second thoughts and leaves a packet of cigarettes on the table. Tiptoes out.

ENTRANCE TO MILITARY HOSPITAL – EL OUED – MORNING

Sliman, sitting on the steps. The Military Hospital forms the fourth side of the quadrangle of the army barracks. A few eucalyptus trees. Captain Junot, accompanied by a French spahi sergeant, walks briskly by.

> JUNOT: Sergeant Ehnni!

62

Sliman gets to his feet, salutes.

> JUNOT: You have no right to be here. The Hospital
> Building and its precincts are out of bounds
> to all other ranks unless in possession of a
> Medical Ordinance. . . . You'd be better off,
> Sergeant, getting your kit together. You've
> been posted to Batna. A convoy is leaving at
> dawn tomorrow. You will accompany it.

Sliman falls forward in a dead faint. Captain Junot turns to
his sergeant.

> JUNOT: Freshen him up with some water. And when
> he can take it in, tell him again he's leaving
> tomorrow at dawn.

The Sergeant throws water over Sliman's face.

QUADRANGLE OF MILITARY HOSPITAL – EL OUED – MONTHS LATER

Isabelle, dressed as a woman, arm in sling, is seated on a
bench under one of the eucalyptus trees. Beside her is
Captain Junot. Two soldiers are escorting a chained prisoner
across the square.

> JUNOT: The Doctor tells me his patient is doing well;
> soon, he says, she'll be able to ride again. I
> have a grey stallion that might tempt you.
> I share your love of fine horses.

Isabelle leans forward, her stick between her knees, to watch
the prisoner, who is her assailant, Abdallah.

> JUNOT: He's being transferred to Constantine for the
> trial; he is unrepentant.
> ISABELLE: However much I search my heart, I can find
> no hatred for him.
> JUNOT: We could ride to Kouinine together, just the
> two of us. The horse is small for a stallion,
> but nimble, nimble. . . .

ISABELLE: Still less can I find contempt for him.

She lights a cigarette without offering Junot one.

JUNOT: We are counting upon your testifying against the accused. An example has to be set. These Arabs are beginning to think they can get away with anything.

Isabelle struggles to her feet.

JUNOT: Miss Eberhardt, I'm more than willing to put in a good word for you, but . . .

She hobbles off with the aid of her stick, cigarette in mouth.

JUNOT: . . . my colleagues in Constantine are not likely to forget how you are here with a Russian passport. They can expel you at the drop of a hat. Without any hope of return!

DOCKS – MARSEILLE – APRIL 1902

Early spring sunshine. Isabelle is among the passengers coming through the Customs. She is wearing a burnous over her shoulders, a wool cap on her head, and she is carrying a bundle. The Welcoming Committee surround her. A lady offers a bouquet. Isabelle is dumbfounded. A lawyer makes a formal speech.

LAWYER: Miss Eberhardt. In the name of the Union for Penal Reform we welcome you to Marseille, while protesting most forcibly against your banishment from the territory of Algeria. By pleading for your assailant at his trial, you showed a humanity that has enraged our authorities. They expelled you because they were ashamed!

Cries of 'Shame! Shame!' Clapping. Isabelle clutches the flowers. The group walk from the pier head towards the street. The Lawyer carries her bundle.

LADY:	By expelling you they admitted defeat. It's a victory!
JOURNALIST:	Would you be willing to give an interview?
ISABELLE:	I can't help you.
LAWYER:	How did the accused react to your intervention?
ISABELLE:	With resignation.
JOURNALIST:	Do you think France will invade Morocco?
ISABELLE:	If it pays them.

A Literary Man takes Isabelle's arm and slows her down so that they are alone for a moment.

LITERARY MAN:	I'm the editor of a review published in Algiers – here's my card. I'll publish anything you write about Algeria, Tunisia, or Morocco.
ISABELLE:	I need money.
LITERARY MAN:	We will pay you.
LADY:	I read a wonderful story by you in the Revue Blanche.

The group arrive at the street and the tramway.

YOUNG LADY:	And you are not worried about the status of women in Islam?
ISABELLE:	You must excuse me, I'm late.
LADY:	We have arranged a little reception for you – it's only ten minutes away in a carriage.
ISABELLE:	I can't. I have an appointment here across the street.
YOUNG WOMAN:	Here?
ISABELLE:	Yes, with the King of Rats.

She takes her bundle and walks away, hunched up and limping.

AUGUSTIN'S KITCHEN – MARSEILLE – EVENING

The apartment is the same except that the seashells have been replaced by bicycle wheels and Hélène, the baby, is now four years old. The bicycle wheels hang from the ceiling near a workbench. Isabelle in her student frock, which looks too young for her, is feeding her niece at the table. Semolina and apricots.

HÉLÈNE: I don't want any more. I want the story of the crocodile.
ISABELLE: The crocodile who swallowed the sun?
HÉLÈNE: Yes, the sun!

Isabelle arranges the contents of the plate to illustrate the story.

ISABELLE: Here's the sun on a dune! Open your mouth. Once there was a crocodile who was so hungry he swallowed the sun. All the plants and animals were sad, sad. They couldn't live.
HÉLÈNE: What did they do?
ISABELLE: They died.
HÉLÈNE: Like Grandpa?
ISABELLE: Yes . . . like Vava.

Isabelle is for a moment lost.

HÉLÈNE: Go on with the story.
ISABELLE: Only the hedgehog didn't cry, because he was thinking.

Augustin comes in with a shopping basket. There is nothing left of the dandy. He sits down at the table and picks up Hélène's glass of water. He takes a bottle of pastis from his basket and pours some into the water. He raises his eyebrows at his sister. She shakes her head.

Hélène gets down from the table and tries to spin one of the suspended bicycle wheels.

AUGUSTIN: Every humiliation we suffer is meticulously prepared.
ISABELLE: Tiny, a happy life, like a classical play, needs unity of time and space.

AUGUSTIN:	Did you have time to look at the papers about the Villa Nuova?
ISABELLE:	No.

Augustin helps himself to another pastis.

AUGUSTIN:	It took me a month to believe. When the Cactophil removed himself from the business scene. . . .
ISABELLE:	Don't talk like that, Tiny.
AUGUSTIN:	When Cactophil died, this scoundrel wrote to me. There's nothing left.
ISABELLE:	You're sure you didn't lose it all at cards?
HÉLÈNE:	What did the hedgehog think, Auntie?
ISABELLE:	The hedgehog was thinking how to get the sun out of the crocodile's belly.

Augustin leaves the table and spins a bicycle wheel.

AUGUSTIN:	That's how the Rostovski family has ended, without a sou, without a penny.
HÉLÈNE:	And hedgehog?
ISABELLE:	He pricked the crocodile so hard with his spikes that the sun fell out. Open your mouth.
AUGUSTIN:	Do you remember the garden and the summer house?
ISABELLE:	So the hedgehog said to all the animals: 'We must stand one on top of the other, high, high, high, 'til we can nail the sun back into the sky!'
HÉLÈNE:	I like the Hedgity Hog.

Augustin spins the wheel again.

AUGUSTIN:	Not a penny! We're dirt like everybody else.

Isabelle takes his hand and caresses it.

SHIP'S DINING ROOM

On the regular crossing from Marseille to Algiers. It is lunchtime and in the crowded First Class dining-room, Lyautey, now a general, and Eugène, now a major, are seated together. The Wine Waiter is attending to them.

LYAUTEY: The Moselle, please waiter. We shall toast the coastline of Algeria. Ah, my Eugène, the sight of that land brings back memories. The beauty of the desert, the beauty of the people . . .

The Wine Waiter pours a small amount of wine into Lyautey's glass.

LYAUTEY: Excellent.

The Waiter fills the glasses. Lyautey proposes a toast.

LYAUTEY: To the new country we are going to make. To our Morocco.
EUGÈNE: Our Morocco. Who says it is ours?
LYAUTEY: This is no time for modesty.

Eugène empties his glass, the Waiter refills it.

EUGÈNE: No time for modesty! Tonkin is a French provincial town stuck in Indo-China.
LYAUTEY: Are you still thinking, my dear, of your little nomad lover?
EUGÈNE: To the Eiffel Tower we will build in the Moroccan desert!

A Waiter brings food.

LYAUTEY: I admire your Isabelle, your reader of Pushkin and the Koran. She has become quite famous. Perhaps notorious is the better word.

Eugène does not touch his plate.

EUGÈNE:	Who was behind the assassination?
LYAUTEY:	In the archives and in the long hallways of the Quai d'Orsay, the rumour arose that she was a cunning and extremely dangerous element.
EUGÈNE:	How stupid can they get?
LYAUTEY:	Bureaucrats never appreciate the beauty of a soul that is true to itself. They considered her a rebel. And, of course, in their small minds they were right. But aren't we all rebels?
EUGÈNE:	No, we are not.
LYAUTEY:	Well, there are moments in love . . . and there are moments in battle when we forget ourselves. Like candles who burn themselves out and bring light to the world.

Eugène drinks.

EUGÈNE:	All we bring are little Eiffel Towers.

SMALL STREET – MARSEILLE – MONTHS LATER

Sliman and Isabelle arm in arm. Sliman, dressed in a suit, looks unwell, with circles under his eyes.

ISABELLE:	Five . . . ten . . . twenty . . . twenty-five francs!
SLIMAN:	How much will it cost?
ISABELLE:	I don't know. Augustin says it shouldn't cost too much, particularly if we take them back the same day, before they close.

They enter a small clothes shop.

CLOTHES HIRE SHOP

The name over the door is Baltounyan.

BALTOUNYAN:	Dresses for a ball?

SLIMAN:	For a wedding.
BALTOUNYAN:	For the lady too?
SLIMAN:	For both of us.
BALTOUNYAN:	Here is the price list.

They study it together.

ISABELLE:	Why don't we get married like we are?
SLIMAN:	It's for the photograph!
ISABELLE:	To put on a fucking mantelpiece!

Baltounyan brings out his ledger.

BALTOUNYAN:	Names, please.
SLIMAN:	Sliman Ehnni and Isabelle Eberhardt.
BALTOUNYAN:	Eberhardt . . . Eberhardt . . . I've heard that name . . . Something . . . Ah . . . the trial in Constantine. Good God, we read about it every day in the papers. It was you?

Isabelle nods and takes Sliman's hand.

BALTOUNYAN:	You behaved, if I may say so, Madame, like a true Christian. Unforgettable. Saintlike. There's no other word for it. Saintlike. Let me find you a dress.

Isabelle and Sliman wait. Baltounyan comes back holding up an extravagant white dress with a veil.

BALTOUNYAN:	You must wear this one!

Sliman anxiously consults the price list. Baltouynyan makes a sign to indicate that money doesn't enter into the affair.

BALTOUNYAN:	Isabelle Eberhardt! Try it on, over there. The honeymoon is where?
SLIMAN:	For honeymoon we say: Seven Fig Days!
BALTOUNYAN:	Are you going to stay in our country?
SLIMAN:	When we are married we can return to Algeria. By marrying me, my wife becomes

French, and with a French passport she can come back to my country.

Isabelle appears in the bridal dress.

> SLIMAN: A flock of sheep would stop grazing to look at you!
> BALTOUNYAN: It's my wedding present – but don't forget to bring it back tomorrow.

SHACK – OUTSKIRTS OF MARSEILLE

Isabelle, in her veil and wedding dress. Sliman in his suit. They have walked several miles from the city, and are tired. A small inlet where there is a broken wooden jetty and a wooden shack. Isabelle pushes open the door. On the floorboards, a thin layer of sand: on the sand, two mats. Some candles. Opposite the door, a huge bunch of mimosa in a rusty bucket.

> ISABELLE: You like it? I spent days working on it. I had to walk a long way to find the sand.
> SLIMAN: Poor Zuiza!
> ISABELLE: No. I knew you were coming. I knew it before you wrote to me. I wanted this hut to be like our home in El Oued.

Isabelle finds a bottle of red wine behind her bundle and places it on the sand in front of Sliman.

> ISABELLE: Bucket after bucket I fetched, but here the sand is dirty. . . . Here the people are lost . . . how long it all takes, what we've been through!
> SLIMAN: You love your Sliman?
> ISABELLE: I love you all the time. Before, After, During. Shit! What does it mean?

Isabelle starts to undo her wedding dress.

> ISABELLE: The best joke of all is: You and I are now

	married! Before the Registrar in the Town Hall. Legal matrimony! What an end!
SLIMAN:	You didn't want us to be married?
ISABELLE:	You are stupid!
SLIMAN:	Stupid! Stupid! You never stop telling me I'm stupid. Why did you always want to go further with me if I'm so stupid?
ISABELLE:	It's so cold here. . . . Maman is dead, Vava is dead. Cactophil is dead . . . he killed himself, you know that? He killed himself with gas. . . . All the family was –

She makes a sign to indicate 'mad'.

SLIMAN:	Drink something!
ISABELLE:	You have four more fucking years in the army!
SLIMAN:	We can go back together now. They can't keep you out – we'll go to Batna together.
ISABELLE:	Batna! The word's like a prison. Worse than Bone!
SLIMAN:	We'll manage somehow.
ISABELLE:	Listen, I have an idea – I've had it before. Let's leave together.
SLIMAN:	Where?
ISABELLE:	We'll die together. To die together is the real wedding.
SLIMAN:	How?
ISABELLE:	Both of us together! We'll go.
SLIMAN:	Have you thought how?

Isabelle searches in her bundle and flourishes Vava's revolver.

ISABELLE:	It's our only inheritance.
SLIMAN:	Do you have any rounds, Zuiza?
ISABELLE:	We'll buy bullets tomorrow. And we'll leave together, the two of us.

Original line drawing by Isabelle Eberhardt

Act 3

MILITARY ENCAMPMENT – MOROCCAN FRONTIER – DUSK – 1904

A small abandoned village near Béni-Ounif, full of soldiers, camp-followers and animals because General Lyautey is assembling his troops in the region. A handful of ruins or never finished buildings – with walls, doorways, courtyards but no roofs – have become at night the improvised meeting place for soldiers, camel drivers and nomads.

Around a bonfire in the open, a number of black Sudanese musicians are heating their drums (to tighten the skin) in the flames. Men are lying on the ground, others sitting, some drinking mint tea. Rifles leaning against the walls. Everything is temporary, and yet an atmosphere of eternal waiting.

Some Legionnaires are sitting, not on the ground, but on boxes, a bottle of alcohol between their feet.

KARL:	The Dane was engaged to be married in Copenhagen.
ENGLISHMAN:	Instead, he's been buried in El Moungar.
ITALIAN:	Zero . . . zero . . . zero . . .
KARL:	To call the column to a halt there, you had to have a brain the size of a split pea!

A Swede is concentratedly taking his pulse.

ENGLISHMAN:	It was like announcing to those cut-throats: Come and do us!
ITALIAN:	Thirty-four who will sing no more.

Silence.

KARL:	You're taking your pulse?
SWEDE:	One hundred and twenty.
KARL:	Paludisme, my friend.
ENGLISHMAN:	What's that?
KARL:	Malaria.

The Sudanese start to play their drums. Music that seems to

come out of the earth: the feet hear it before the ears. A number of Mozkahzni begin to move with the music, but they are not yet dancing. Three Old Women sit on the ground, backs to a wall. Seated beside them, Isabelle, dressed as Mahmoud. A Camel Driver bends down to one of the Old Women.

CAMEL DRIVER: Ten years ago in Duveyrier, remember?
OLD WOMAN: Liar! Nothing bad happened between us.
CAMEL DRIVER: Bad! Of course not. There's nothing so good as that in the world, nothing so good.

Through the dust and the billowing robes of the men dancing, a Mokhazni with a red burnous and black beard is staring at an unveiled woman in the doorway. Very deliberately he passes his hand over his beard, downward. The woman almost imperceptibly shakes her head. An Old Woman leans towards Isabelle.

OLD WOMAN: Do you know what the hand on the beard like that says? It's a message and it says 'I'll let 'em shave off my beard, sign of my manhood, if I don't have the chance of lying with you tonight.' Do you miss him?

Isabelle nods her head.

OLD WOMAN: The eyes of your beloved are two stars. On his chest are spring roses.

Isabelle plays with the sand between her fingers.

LANDSCAPE – BENI OUNIF – AFTERNOON

A desert landscape, very different from that of El Oued. It is jagged instead of undulating. Isabelle and two children who lead her by the hand are walking fast between the rocks. They show her a grey camel lying in its death agony. From its grey eyes, tears. (*Camels do weep.*) A Woman, unveiled, barefoot, rifle slung over her shoulder, passes by.

ISABELLE: In the name of God, the only God, do you have a bullet?

WOMAN: With the men gone and the dog bandits of every colour everywhere, would –

Without finishing her sentence, she hands over the rifle. Isabelle fires and dispatches the camel.

ISABELLE: Shall I tell you how it is? Adam says: 'I'm not the father of the world, I've never seen paradise. Lead me to God!'

MILITARY ENCAMPMENT

A Legionnaire is playing his accordion. One of the three old women is in her usual place, with Isabelle seated beside her. On the ground between them a plate of plain couscous.

OLD WOMAN: Last month, Fathima Zohra's lover was shot by a *dijouch* and yet tonight, they say, she will dance.

ISABELLE: Dancing to an absence is hard.

OLD WOMAN: My eyes can't see . . . your voice tells me you are not well.

ISABELLE: Only fever. For days on end. Soon I'll go back to my Sliman. He will look after me. It's been too long. The eyes of my beloved are two stars. On his chest are spring roses.

A voice shouts from beyond the ruins.

Isabelle strides to the archway that looks out onto the stones of the plain. The Man who was shouting is on a small, galloping white horse.

MAN: They have killed my brother! They have killed my brother!

The horse is without bridle or saddle, and the rider is barefoot. When the horse stops, the Man falls to the ground and rolls there, as if in a fit, wringing his hands, and

79

repeating that his brother is dead. Isabelle crouches beside him, places one hand on his back. The Man stops his contortions and sobs.

Isabelle walks away from him and the encampment. The Legionnaire Karl addresses his Swedish friend.

> KARL: First of all he's a woman. Secondly, she's a writer. Thirdly, because she's a bit mad, the villagers here and the nomads believe she has baraka.
> SWEDE: Baraka?
> KARL: A touch of God.
> SWEDE: Have you seen her knocking back aguardiente? Jesus! She could drink me under the table.

Fathima Zohra begins to dance. A hundred men watch. Green veil with silver strands, white bodice and violet velvet dress. On the faces of the men, Arab and European, the same expression. Not of desire, but of recollection.

> SWEDE: Look over there, by the archway. He's come back and he's watching Fathima dance.
> KARL: Who?
> SWEDE: Your one with the baraka.

QUARTERMASTER'S STORES – BATNA – EVENING

Sliman, in uniform but without a cap, is standing behind a counter; it is the section of the stores that deals with uniforms. On the door of a cupboard beside him is the framed wedding photograph from Marseille. A line of soldiers waiting at the counter. Each one presents a paper. Sliman stamps it with a rubber stamp and then hands over the appropriate service issue. A belt, a pair of boots, a tunic. The last soldier served, Sliman locks up and leaves with a wrapped package under his arm.

CAFE NEAR BARRACKS – BATNA

The cafe is full of men, Arab and European. Sliman enters
and sits at his usual table, the wrapped package on his
knees. The other men, while drinking, are continually looking
at a building across the street. Its windows are shuttered, its
double doors closed and barred.

A trader approaches Sliman.

TRADER:	How many francs?
SLIMAN:	Fifty a pair.
TRADER:	You know where you are?
SLIMAN:	Batna.
TRADER:	I'll give you ten.

The Trader discreetly opens the paper of Sliman's package
and looks inside at the boots.

SLIMAN:	Boots manufactured in France!
TRADER:	A friend got a pair of army issue for eight francs.
SLIMAN:	Not of this quality.

Two Spahis stop by the table. In the building opposite the
shutters are being opened by a woman: it is the town brothel.

FIRST SPAHI:	You never come with us, Sergeant.
SECOND SPAHI:	Sergeant Ehnni is married.
FIRST SPAHI:	Is his wife at home?
SECOND SPAHI:	No she isn't. He can't keep her at home!

Sliman raises his arm, but controls his anger. The Spahis
leave.

TRADER:	Twenty for the pair – take it or leave it.
SLIMAN:	One hundred francs more and I'll be able to join my wife. I'll give you three pairs for a hundred.
TRADER:	Four!

The barred doors of the brothel open, and men hurry out of the café to run across the street.

SLIMAN: At this table tomorrow with cash?
TRADER: Four pairs; one hundred. Agreed.

The Trader leaves. The Waiter comes to wipe the table. Three Military Policemen appear from behind the bar. Two seize Sliman, the third opens the package. The Policemen handcuff Sliman and lead him off.

LANDSCAPE – BENI-OUNIF – MIDDAY

A small, irregular white building, shaped like a beehive. A low doorway without a door, no windows. Isabelle's horse tethered outside, head protected from the sun with a cloth.

Inside the building are two large wooden chests, as high as tables. These mark the graves where a marabout and his wife were buried, four generations ago.

Isabelle, who has lit two candles, is praying. Something surprises her. Hesitantly, she gets to her feet, teeters around one of the chests. On his back, an Old Man, eyes open and staring.

ISABELLE: What are you doing here?
OLD MAN: I'm dying.
ISABELLE: Perhaps your hour has not come.
OLD MAN: Once I was able to watch the sheep with my children's children. When I became too weak even for that, my sons carried me here, and it is here that the angels of death will come to fetch me.
ISABELLE: Which is your village?

The Old Man shuts his eyes. Isabelle leaves the tomb, mounts and rides away. Then, she slumps forward onto the neck of her horse.

FRENCH ARMY H.Q. – EARLY AFTERNOON

Many tents. A French sergeant has already noticed the odd
behaviour of an approaching horseman and has sent out men
to investigate. General Lyautey comes to the entrance of his
luxurious marquee. Soldiers are leading the horse by its
bridle. The rider is apparently unconscious in the saddle.

> LYAUTEY: What have you got there?

A few steps and he recognizes Isabelle.

> LYAUTEY: Put him on my bed.

The Sergeant does not hide his surprise. Lyautey turns and
walks back into his tent. Isabelle, supported under each arm,
legs limp, raises her head for a moment.

> SERGEANT: Get on with it, you heard the General's
> order, place this wog on the General's bed!

MARQUEE OF GENERAL LYAUTEY

The large, high tent is furnished like a room, with carpets,
cushions, a period dining-table with chairs, fine china,
elaborate paraffin lamps. The predominant colour is deep red.
The tent entrance is open and we see a Sentry on guard
outside. Lyautey lights a cigarette from his 'eternal' flame.
Isabelle is lying on the bed, covered with blankets. She stirs.

> LYAUTEY: How do you feel?
> ISABELLE: Done for.
> LYAUTEY: Getting better is a matter of willpower.
> You're going to get better, I haven't the
> slightest doubt. You have every reason to get
> better. The Arab Bureau is leaving you alone
> these days. You're free!
> ISABELLE: My husband is sick. . . .
> LYAUTEY: So you really are married?
> ISABELLE: He's sick, he still has four more years to

serve in the army, he's a Sergeant with the Spahi, Sliman Ehnni.

Lyautey turns to the Sentry.

> LYAUTEY: I want to know the whereabouts of Sergeant Sliman Ehnni.

He approaches the bed.

> LYAUTEY: Everything will be arranged. They thought I was at death's door six months ago, and look at me now.
>
> ISABELLE: You and I don't lead the same life.
>
> LYAUTEY: Come, come, a little less of your oriental fatalism. You have won the confidence of the Lords of the Desert. They listen to you and you will be able to persuade them that it is in their interest to go along with us. You and I are going to bring Peace and Order to this poor land.

He realizes she is asleep. Approaching the bed, he lightly strokes her forehead. As he stands there, a young Military Doctor arrives.

OUTSIDE MARQUEE

The Sentry salutes.

> SENTRY: Sergeant Sliman Ehnni has been sentenced to six years of military prison in Batna.
>
> LYAUTEY: Order him to be released immediately.

As the Sentry steps away, the Military Doctor comes out of the tent.

> DOCTOR: A typical case of yellow fever. With good hospital treatment, the patient will recover. What I am much more anxious about is the patient's general condition. The patient has

84

the physique of somebody thirty years older, due, I'd say, to every kind of excess. After all, she's a woman –

LYAUTEY: Woman! She has the strength of three men! I want her sent to Ain Sefra tomorrow, with a special train and a nurse. See to it, Captain, and detail Major Eugène Letord to accompany her.

DESERT TRAIN – NEXT DAY

A railway wagon, which has been converted for transporting the seriously wounded. Several beds, then a white partition with a door in the middle with a red cross on it. Isabelle lies on one of the beds, eyes shut. Eugène is sitting on the next bed, bending over her. The train goes slowly. The tracks are badly laid.

ISABELLE: Stop the cocks crowing, Cactophil, stop them. Please . . . I can't sleep.

Eugène wipes her lips, changes the towel on her forehead.

ISABELLE: The sun needs a nail. . . .

A Nursing Sister comes through the door with a white box. She has difficulty in walking as the train sways.

EUGÈNE: She is delirious, Nurse.
NURSE: You insisted upon staying with her, Major.

Time passes. Isabelle opens her eyes and sees Eugène for the first time.

ISABELLE: You!

She tries to sit up, and arrange her hair.

EUGÈNE: Don't worry. It's only me.

ISABELLE:	Where are we?
EUGÈNE:	On the way to the hospital in Ain Sefra. Everything is all right. You'll be looked after. Your husband is coming.
ISABELLE:	When?
EUGÈNE:	In a few days.
ISABELLE:	When?
EUGÈNE:	In three or four days, for sure.
ISABELLE:	I don't want to go to a hospital. I'll get better more quickly with him, but not in a hospital. You know me, Eugene, I can't bear prisons.
EUGÈNE:	Yes, that's something I do know.
ISABELLE:	Thank you.
EUGÈNE:	You're funny.
ISABELLE:	Not always. Not always, my sweetheart. But tell me about you.
EUGÈNE:	My mother died. I've inherited the family property. Vineyards, forests . . .
ISABELLE:	So you're rich?
EUGÈNE:	Do you need money?
ISABELLE:	I did, but no more now. Tell me about you –
EUGÈNE:	I don't believe in anything, Isabelle. I'll get out of the army and go home and busy myself with forestry and livestock and my tenants. In the evenings I'll read books and sit by the fire . . . and this will be my way of remaining faithful to you.
ISABELLE:	There is so little to remain faithful to, look at me! Look at me, I'm a ruin.

One of Isabelle's feet is sticking out beyond the blanket.
Eugène holds her ankle as he arranges the blanket.

EUGÈNE:	Do you remember the trouble we had finding a pair of shoes for you? Do you remember? It was in Bone. You remember Bone? I still want you, Isabelle, yes I still want you.
ISABELLE:	It could be Death you want, my sweet one. Death can lure us all into bed.

She closes her eyes. Suddenly she tries to get up.

86

ISABELLE: Promise me, Eugène, promise me you won't take me to hospital. I want to wait for him in a house.

HOUSE IN AIN SEFRA

The town is on two levels: the upper town of military barracks, and the lower town of small houses following the curve of a river bed. Apart from a few stagnant pools, the river bed is dry.

A small house with a flat roof arranged as a terrace with a shelter of rushes. There is an outside staircase. In the street shops, goats and children.

Supported on either side by Eugène and the Nurse, Isabelle climbs the stairs to the roof terrace.

EUGÈNE: This is your house.

From the roof they look at the wadi and the few pools of water.

ISABELLE: And God divided the land from the waters – that's the first condition for a home, isn't it? Thank you, Eugène, thank you.

ROOM IN HOUSE – AIN SEFRA – A FEW DAYS LATER

A small white room with a beaten earth floor and a window giving onto the river bed. A table, some stools, a cupboard. On the table, some fruit. Isabelle's bed is a mattress on the floor. She is folding down the white sheets of the bed.

She straightens up, hesitates, goes to a cupboard, and then across to a mirror hanging beside the window. There, with great ceremony, she makes herself up. She paints her lips bright red. She is dressed in a white djellaba. She ties a white kerchief around her head. She blackens her eyebrows with khol. She looks out of the window and sees Sliman, walking down the riverbed towards the house. She cries out and hobbles towards the door, smiling.

ROOM IN HOUSE – AIN SEFRA – NIGHT

Isabelle and Sliman are lying on the white bed. Sliman pulls the kerchief off her head. Isabelle shuts her eyes. Sliman caresses her forehead.

> ISABELLE: Take the things out of my bundle, Zuizou, we're home. At last we're home.

Sliman gets up, undoes her bundle and starts to put away her possessions.

He arranges a small pile of clothes on a shelf in the cupboard. He hangs up her 'student' dress on a nail in the wall. He puts her notebooks on another shelf in the cupboard. With the revolver, he hesitates for a moment, then places it on the table, near a half-eaten loaf of bread.

Lastly he takes out a handful of screwed-up envelopes and papers. From among the papers a drawing of a garden in a palm grove falls on the floor. He looks around and sees the bread, which gives him an idea. He chews a little of the dough, presses it between his fingers, and uses it as an adhesive to stick the drawing to the wall.

TERRACE OF HOUSE – AIN SEFRA – A FEW NIGHTS LATER

Moonlight. Stars. On the flat roof, Isabelle and Sliman are sleeping beneath sheep skins. Sliman's face is buried against her shoulder. Isabelle is looking at the night sky.

> SLIMAN: You're thinking?
> ISABELLE: Yes.
> SLIMAN: What about?
> ISABELLE: I'm thinking about our life. Perhaps it's because I was so close to death, within a hair's breadth, perhaps this is why I feel so much the pain of life and why I need it, this hurting life, like I need you, Zuizou.

TERRACE – AIN SEFRA – DAWN

On the roof of rushes heavy raindrops. Isabelle and Sliman
are asleep in each other's arms. The noise of the rain
awakens Sliman. He slips from under the sheepskins, puts a
burnous over his shoulders and goes down the outside
staircase to enter the room below.

ROOM IN HOUSE – AIN SEFRA – DAWN

Sliman is peeling an orange to take to Isabelle. The drawing
stuck to the wall falls to the floor. He stares at it. There is the
noise of rushing water. He goes to the door and sees a tidal
flood advancing down the river bed.

RIVER BED – AIN SEFRA – DAWN

Sliman has been swept several hundred feet downstream. He
manages to grab the branch of a tree and pull himself out of
the water. At this moment he sees their house carried away.

  SLIMAN: Isabelle, I-sa-belle, *Iiii–saaa–belle* . . .

MARQUEE OF GENERAL LYAUTEY – NOVEMBER 1904

The General is standing by his table on which is laid out a
large map of Algeria and Morocco. Near him stands Eugène.
They are alone.

Lyautey walks down the tent towards the bed. Beside it, a
lacquered trunk with painted dragons from Indo-China. On
the lid of this trunk are papers and notebooks, many pages
have been damaged by water and mud. Isabelle's revolver is
on top of them.

  LYAUTEY: We found her under the ruins of the house. I
     gave the order to search everywhere for
     everything of hers that could be found. The
     search went on for two days and two nights,
     in shifts. One must always think of posterity,
     Eugène, always. . . .